Twisted Love...

Caroline J. Robison

iUniverse, Inc.
New York   Bloomington

iUniverse books may be ordered through booksellers or by contacting:

iUniverse
1663 Liberty Drive
Bloomington, IN 47403
www.iuniverse.com
1-800-Authors (1-800-288-4677)

Because of the dynamic nature of the Internet, any Web addresses or links contained in this book may have changed since publication and may no longer be valid. The views expressed in this work are solely those of the author and do not necessarily reflect the views of the publisher, and the publisher hereby disclaims any responsibility for them.

ISBN: 978-1-4502-2077-4 (sc)
ISBN: 978-1-4502-2078-1 (hc)
ISBN: 978-1-4502-2079-8 (ebook)

Printed in the United States of America

iUniverse rev. date: 03/18/2010

Dedications

I dedicate this book to my best friend Michelle Holly Hall and to my other Best friend Shannon Emily Marques, you guys have been there for me since day one and until the end and I love you guys with all my heart. I also dedicate this to My father and My mother (Moomoo) and My sister Kristy for they have always supported me in everything that I did and helped me along the way as well. I love you guys and always will.

Miracle. . ...

The sun was burning red with its scorching rays slowly starting
to expand and cover the earth, as soon as it began to fall from
the earth in a matter of time you could see that everything that
it had brought back to life had changed and as it disappeared
from the world it seemed like it was as if the whole world was
bleeding with passion, changing everything in the day. After a
couple of hours the night slowly began to come alive as the
moon was starting to break free and the sun had set, the moon
slowly started to move up from the end of the earth. But as the
world started to rest from the events from the previous day, not
knowing of the problems from the rest of the world, in a small
town called Morehead City, North Carolina. The trees stood
tall, the air was clean and fresh with every day that passed, and
the beach was glowing with excitement as summer covered the
air with the feeling of being able to be free and have fun filled
the town. Where the family lived was a nice area and peaceful,
the house was white with black shutters. The house was between
two others that were old and strong with white and shutters of
their choice. With houses everywhere and shopping places not
that far from houses and other businesses, the town was very
peaceful and relaxing to those that have lived their whole lives.
A couple miles down the road was a large bridge and then a road
that led you to another smaller bridge that entered another part
of a town named Beaufort and with this gave you access to
others businesses and restaurants and shops and beaches that
could be a lifelong vacation place. There was many things that
could be done here and even outside of the city but Cars drove
on the streets on the two way highways that lead cars in one

direction and then in another, but also you could see cars heading to their other destinations on the each side of the road. But as the morning began and everything going like life normally does not knowing what the day will bring, That morning the blue skies were drawing the Kids closer to the beaches and to begin their freedom as they started to splash in the water with their parents close by and everyone sun bathing on the sand enjoying the weather. But as life went on no one knew that in a near hospital a mother was about to give birth to her only child, when an old woman named Mrs. Lucinda Jones that was considered a witch came into her hospital room and laid her hand on the mother's stomach and said, "Ahh, Danger will always find her but she will have the power to outlive us all" The old woman left after her message and the mother laid there confused and not sure what the old woman meant by that. But The mother sat there in pain in her sides and back while her little girl got ready inside of her, After a couple of minutes the doctor came in and was throwing out orders to the nurses and family and then turned to her and said "okay, father and grandmother I need you to hold her feet and legs and dear you need to push" The mother pushed with all her might and after pushing and pushing the baby girl came out freely and the doctor was holding her wrapped in rags covered in blood. She gave the little girl to the mother for a little bit while she tried to fix up the mother but while she was trying to fix her, pain hit her so bad that she almost dropped the baby girl. The doctor took her a way and gave her to the nurses and soon the mother was being thrashed back into the hospital bed from the pain and it taking over as the doctors was trying to fix her and rush her to the emergency room. She was having problems breathing and the blood would not stop flowing from her and the pain was even stronger than before. The doctor's did everything that they could but she hem ridged and died quickly and soon she could feel the darkness coming over her and she knew that she was leaving her little girl and her husband behind, even though she tried to fight it and be there for her little girl but death came over her and soon she was gone. The father stood there watching as the love of his life was leaving the world and he was on his own and didn't know what to do or feel but he did know that he was sad and hurt for the loss of his wife but he knew that he was going to have to be strong for Michelle and so he made plans with her grandmother so that she could watch her when he was at work. They tried living their life the best that they could as the days got harder and the nights even worse, the father continued to have dreams and nightmares of his beloved wife dying and knew that his daughter was a miracle and so he tried to be there for her the best that he could. He felt that his world was going for the worst as his job was getting harder and busy, as he owned his own construction company. He was working long hours and not being able to spend any time with Michelle like he wanted to but he knew that things would get better or so he hoped. He planned the funeral with family and friends by his side at the nearest grave yard and family and friends gathered at his small house that was white with black shutters. He knew that it was going to be hard to be able to sit there with everyone as he knew that his wife was not there but he stuck it up and as they brought food and gathered around talking about his wife and how she was a wonderful woman and friend. He knew that with them it would be better than it was right that moment. But after awhile he knew that he had to be there for his daughter and even though she was young and didn't understand, he wanted to make sure that she knew that he loved her and would do anything for her. Before the funeral they had a service at the closest church he could find, he wasn't a very religious man but his wife was so he tried to do the best that he could and then a day later after his beloved wife was pulled down into the earth, he walked away standing tall feeling that everything will be okay. As time passed and life seemed to get harder and then better he realized that his daughter was special she read at the age of 2 and talked as well. He loved her so much and everyday when he came home he knew that she was the only reason why he was kept alive. After a couple of years her grandmother passed away and so the father was getting discouraged and knew that life was going to be harder than before but he sucked it in and decided that he was going to hire a babysitter because she was only 5 years old and then one night without warning the weather was bad and on his way home to his daughter his tires lost grip of the road and spun him around several times before it stopped but when it finally stopped spinning him around he thought to himself okay I can do this but then he realized that the car was hanging off the cliff and when he tried to balance the car it stilted forward and before he could stop it, it lunged forward and went down the hill hitting everything in its path as if someone was doing it on purpose and when it finally hit the ground, the father was crushed against the steering wheel and then once he hit it he was thrown through the windshield and landed a few feet from the car and the only thing that was running through his head was the memory of his wife and daughter and that he hoped he did everything that he could for them and that he loved him because he knew that these were the last seconds of his life and with this when he hit the ground he slowly saw everything flash before him and shortly after that he died instantly. In the distance of the night a figure came out of the trees and took his fingers and checked his pulse to make sure he was dead. And when this figure was satisfied he traveled up the hill to the house where the girl was living. His goal was to take her and raise her with his family as a part of their family because they knew who she was and knew that she was one of them. But before he reached the house, He saw that the cops had showed up and that meant that someone called the cops and that they saw him as well. So, he kept walking and would deal with them later, as well as the girl and so he kept walking and disappeared into the woods near a house that was a couple doors down from the house where the girl was. He knew that he could go in and take her if he wanted to but it was a hard risk that he wasn't willing to take so he would deal with it later but he knew that he had to take care of the people that saw him so he focused and saw within the neighborhood that a woman was peeking through her house looking at the direction of where he was. So, he thought okay what should I do to take care of her and then it came to him, he focused into his thoughts and within a couple of seconds he heard the woman scream as she was faced with her only fear and that was death. He disappeared into the night as the cops took the little girl away and into the hands of the state but then shortly after that she was sent into foster care and she went through many homes and even though she was little she was always distancing herself from people and sometimes she would act out because she didn't want to be with anyone but her real family, She was told that she had no more family but she knew that she did and so fought them every chance she had. Soon she was 5 and was sent to this house that had two their kids and they would make fun of her and make her do things that she didn't like, for instance they would make her wait on them hand and foot and sometimes they would blame everything on her and so she did something that she never thought was in her and she said out loud that was hateful and wrong but at the time she didn't care and so she wished that the kids would get what they deserved and so not long after she said those words she saw the kids vanish before her eyes and so she grabbed her stuff and ran away. She took off not caring where she ended up or what happened and as she walked down the streets, she saw the car that was going to take her back to the Child Care and so she tried to hide but they spotted her and picked her up and as days went by she tried to get out of there but never had the luck and then before she knew it she was 10 and finally got her chance to break free and After dealing with all those years of not knowing who her parents were but finding out that they died and that her father killed himself or so she was told and dealing with the loss of her parents even though she didn't understand she could feel the pain in her heart and mind. But after a while she got over it and when she ran away she was walking down the streets taking care of herself and basically living on the streets she ran into a woman that was beautiful and so sweet and calm and she was about to get in her car and when they locked eyes that afternoon. The woman stopped what she was doing and walked over to her and said, "Honey, You look horrible are you okay?" Michelle didn't know what to say to this but then she said, "Yes, I have been walking for some time and would like something to eat and maybe a shower' The woman said, "Come on honey, You can come into our house and take a shower and I will fix you something to eat" Michelle smiled and then said, "Thank you" The woman was very nice and friendly and Michelle liked her at some point and when she entered the big house she felt like was walking in a mansion. It had white walls that were taller than an Elephant and there was stairs on one side of the house and the other from the kitchen to get to the upstairs and she felt like a princess for once in her life. She sat down and the woman made her a sandwich and gave her a coke and then Michelle realized that the woman was observing her. She smiled and then began to eat, the woman looked at her and then said, "Honey what is your name? And where are your parents?" Michelle knew that this was going to happen and she didn't want to tell her but she liked this woman and so she said, "Well, My parents died when I was born and so I have been sent to many foster homes and places that have mistreated me and so I ran away so that I could get away from it all" When she finished the woman gasped and then said, "Well, honey you can stay here as long as you want too" Michelle smiled at this and then said, "Thank you, I would like that" The woman said, "Well, after you eat take a shower and there should be some clothes that are in the room next to the bathroom that might fit you and then you and I can go shopping for other things if you would like" Michelle unsure at first and then nodded and then said, "Thank you" The woman nodded and then took out her phone and called her husband and when he answered she said, "Honey, I was about to leave the house when a young girl stop in my drive way and she looked bruised and very bad and so she is staying with us because her parents died when she was little and her foster care families mistreat her, so I am going to take her shopping and get her some things and then I can come in later after I can see if the neighbors will watch her" She listened to his response and then said, "Okay, Honey see you then" She hung up the phone and then turned to Michelle and said, "It is all settled you will be with us, and I hope that one day you will consider us family but we will not push you in away. She live with them for awhile before she felt like it was her family but it didn't take too long because they treated her like their daughter and soon after they adopted her she was. And they tried to be there for her and help her and raise her the best that they could since the mother could not have children and they were glad when they found her at a young age but for a while she resented them and didn't want to be with them or their family but as years passed and she accepted that her parents were longer living, she found that the people that adopted her cared for her and soon she did too. So, she tried to make it right for them and make it easy for them and then she found that she could not have asked for a better step family and she tried to live her life the best way that she could and after 10 years of unsure answers and of not knowing her real parents and remembering everything that she went through she grew up knowing nothing but her parents that she had now. Even though she was a young girl and living with her new parents, she realized that she was having these strange dreams that were dark and unfocused and she has had them since she was eight but never told anyone.

Changed Life. . ...

Now at the age of 15 she has noticed that her dreams have changed with her and she has seen different people in them and what they are thinking and feel their emotions and has found that she can see them and help them by thinking and change the situation when it gets bad. But the main thing for her is that she doesn't understand why she has this gift or where it came from and what this means, but as time goes by she knows that she was meant for this to happen and that someone wanted her to be able to help those. She was A young girl at the age of 15 years old and named Michelle Emily Hallmar and her life had changed a lot and today was her first day of her second year of high school and she was walking down the street on her way to school feeling like everything in her life was playing out, the way that it should be and her mom and dad were doing well with their business and her grades were better than ever. She went to a typical high school named Havelock High, The building was old and long, the walls were off white and tan colored. When you walked through the two sets of double doors at the entrance way you can see to your right the cafeteria and to your right the main office. There was a hallway to the left of the office and when you walked straight from the doors another hallway that had classes to them as well. She walked down the hall to the bathroom that was at the end of the showcase that was on the right in front of the cafeteria and saw that nothing had changed and that the doors were removed from the bathrooms because students would smoke and do all kinds of crazy things in them. She hurried to the bathroom and then when she was done and washed her hands she walked to her right to join her friends in the cafeteria and saw how many kids were there. They were talking away and not even seeing a couple of the teachers and the principle and the assistant principle that sat in the front watching the students before class started. As she sat there talking and chatting away with her friends a thought came to her and it was that she still had about two years left before she would graduate but she didn't care because her friends were there for her. Well, the few she had anyway, there was Carla Fox that was 15, Jenny Smith that was 16, and her best Friend Kat Benton that was 18. But as the summer came to an end went by so fast she felt like her time was running out to finding true love, she had been in many relationships before this new school year started and as she remembered them there was Arnold Bates that was nice and she thought that she was in love with him but he cheated on her for a girl named Maxine Aiken and there was David Edison that was just too perfect for her and in the end he left to go back home before the year was up, The last guy she dated was Chance Bassington and he was the best thing except towards the end she found out that he was arrested for killing someone and even though she was scared but at the same time she wasn't after that she ended it and has been by herself since then not wanting to get hurt again or to open her heart to no one. Her new parents were always worried about her because she kept falling for the ones that were bad or strange or just not the type that they thought was good for her. But she went on after each one and tried to move on and live the life the best that she could. But even though she hasn't been able to meet the person that she wants to spend it with, her parents kept telling her that she had time for that. She knows the truth though because she was not like the other girls, she didn't have style or beauty she dressed casual with jeans and sneakers and was average for everything. She knew that she would be a lone for a long time but she was okay with that because if no one liked her for her then she wasn't going to waste her time with any of them. Her life was about to change and with it she could only have dreamed for the outcome but with this change it destroys everything that she loved and cared about. As she was thinking this sitting with her friends waiting for the bell to ring, she saw from the corner of her eye a medium height boy that was dressed in jeans and T-shirt that was blue and his shoes were regular sneakers but his hair was blacker then night and his eyes were dark as well but she could not see them. She gasped and didn't realize that she had done it out loud. Her girl Carla looked at her and then laughed when she realized that Michelle was drooling over the boy that walked by. Carla shakes her back to reality and said, "Michelle that is Timmy Oxford, he is 16 and is new here, he moved here from Miami, Florida and will be here until the end of high school so I have been told." Michelle looked at Carla and then said, "I need to know him" Carla laughed and then without hesitating she called, "Hey Timmy" Michelle turned bright red and tried to hush Carla by putting her hand over her mouth but it was too late. Timmy turned around and when he saw Carla he waved and then slowly walked over. Michelle could see him better now and her heart started to jump higher and higher into her throat. Timmy looked at her and his eyes told her that he was unsure what to do. He walked over and sat down across from Michelle and then took her hand to shake it and said, "HI, I'm Timmy" She blushed and then said, "I'm Michelle" He smiled and then Carla said, "Timmy my girl here wants to know more about you" Michelle slugged Carla and said, "Thanks Carla" Timmy laughed and said, "OH, well ask away" Michelle didn't know what to say or do" But then she turned to Carla and said, " How do you know him?" Carla laughed and said, "Me and Timmy have a few classes together and I had to show him around but your safe because I know you like him" Michelle blushed and said, "Thanks Carla" Carla laughed and said, "No problem" Carla turned around and started to talk to a boy that was next to her and then Michelle turned back to Timmy and blushed even brighter but she was nervous and didn't know what to do But she took a deep breath and asked him about his life in Florida and his family and without cause or hesitation he answered every question. He told her that his mother married the meanest man in the world and that he was a drunk and beat her every chance he got. He told her that they moved here because his mother got a job offer, and his real father wanted him to live with him in Atlanta, Georgia but he knew that his mother needed him so he moved with her. He also told her that he hoped that his stepfather would have stayed in Florida but he refused to and so he came with them. He told her many things that she was surprised that he would be so open with her about but she listened until he was finished. So, she felt that he deserved the same in return and so she told him that she was adopted since she was a young kid and that her parents were dead, her mother died when she was born giving birth to her and her father was murdered for a reason that she does not know but intends to find out. Then she told him that her adopted parents were rich and owned many businesses that were all over the world and so they were gone for the most of the time but she didn't mind because it gave her peace and let her deal with life the way that she wanted too. She was so afraid that he would judge her and she was also nervous because she thought that she was giving him too much information, but she had this feeling that she could trust him and that he had lived a hard life like she did. She was shocked to find that they felt a connection after awhile of being able to tell each other secrets and trusting each other even though they had just met they knew that there was a reason that they had met that day and so As they walked each other to each class and talked about each other and their family she learned that his real father and mother were smart people and that his mother planned on staying here. She also learned that her body and mind wanted to know each fear, every emotion and much more that he had. By the end of the day they were having normal conversations about hobbies and desires and likes and dislikes. He walked her home and when they walked up the steps of her house she slowly walked to the door and waited for him to follow her and when he did she couldn't help but smile and then as she approached her door, she turned and said, "Timmy do you want to come in?" Timmy smiled and said, "Will your parents mind?" Michelle laughed but she knew that since she just met him and was not sure that she should do this, but at the same time he seemed harmless but she had to be sure first and so she said, "Timmy, I can trust you right?" He looked at her and then he realized what she was getting at and then he smiled and said, "Yes, You can trust me and I will or would never do anything to hurt you or your parents" She smiled and said, "Okay, well they aren't here; remember I told you they won't be until next week" Timmy laughed and said, "Oh, right I forgot well I would be honored to then." Michelle didn't normally do this but for some reason she trusted him and liked him. He walked in and looked around the house and by his face she could tell that he loved it. She took his hand and said, "Why don't we fix something to eat, and we can sit by the pool and talk some more" Timmy nodded and then followed her and she dragged him to the kitchen. He was looking all around the house and said, "Wow, this is so beautiful" Michelle laughed and said, "My mother did it" Timmy nodded in understanding and then they quickly made some sandwiches and she picked up a bag of chips as they walked out to the patio and sat down in the lounge chairs that were outside by the pool. He sat next to her as they ate their food, and as they were silent she could feel this intense feeling that made her want to touch him. She tried to resist it because she barely knew him but at the same time she felt like she did know him for the longest time. She kept seeing glimpses of images of things of his life that he went through and what he had to face every day, and even though he didn't know what she was or what she could do. Which she wanted to keep it that way for now anyway, she watched each thought of his and glimpse of his fear and his life and it made her sad, She smiled at the thoughts of her and how he really liked her and wanted to spend every minute with her even though they had just met but he knew in his heart that she was the one he was looking for and she made him feel safe and happy for the first time. But then it would switch to his mother and always getting hit for things that were not her fault or him getting hit for things that were not his fault and it made her want to wrap her arms around him and his mother to protect them from this evil man. But she also saw that this man had been doing this for a long time and she saw that when he got older he took professional classes that would help him defend himself and save his mother so she knew that he could fight and take care of himself but she still wanted to protect him and his mother and as she was thinking this. She felt this urge to speak out of anger and frustration and it came out of nowhere, she got so angry towards this man, that she didn't even know that she was doing it or what she said but as it came out it was like she saw herself say it but she could not stop either way and so she said, "I'll kill him if he hurts you or your mother again" She stopped and put her hand up to her mouth and gasped out load. Timmy looked at her and said, "Where did that come from?" Michelle blushed and said, "I don't know Timmy, I'm sorry It just came out" Timmy looked down at the ground and said, "Michelle no one has ever said anything like that to me, I feel like I can trust you and that you feel my pain and for some reason I feel like this is all a dream and that when I wake up my life will be normal" Michelle couldn't take it anymore and so she knelt in front of him and wrapped her arms around him and said, "Oh, Timmy I wish I could make your life normal and to take away the pain so that you could be happy and be safe" Timmy wrapped his arms around her even tighter and said, "Thank you Michelle" They were wrapped around each other for awhile and then she slowly released him and when she let him go, he released her as well and she looked at him and said, "Timmy, I will always be here for you no matter what" Timmy pushed a smile and then said, "Thanks, I will always be here for you no matter what too" They smiled at each other and realized that they were done with their food and so he put his plate and hers on top of each other and moved it to the side. He turned and realized that she was looking at him, he smiled and said, "You know you have beautiful eyes" She blushed and knew that he was trying to change the subject but she knew that he needed this and so she said, "That's all that is beautiful on me" He looked at her and said, "What do you mean?" Michelle took a deep breath and then said, "Timmy every guy that I have been with as either just wanted sex from me or used me or hurt me and so I have found that I am not the prettiest girl that walked this planet and I have accepted it." Timmy listened and then when she was done he turned to her and held her face into his hands and said, "Michelle I have never met anyone like you and your wrong, those guys were idiots and they let go of the most beautiful creature that has ever walked the earth." Michelle turned even redder and then hugged him and he wrapped his arms around her even tighter. She looked up at him and said, "Thanks" He smiled and said, "No Problem". They laughed and he kissed her on the forehead. He stopped what he was doing because he thought that it was the wrong move to make, but Michelle didn't move or anything so he rested his chin on the top of her head. Timmy tried to fight the urge but couldn't take it no more, he knew that she was the one that he was looking for and so he said, "Michelle, I know that we just met and all but I was wondering if you would like to be friends and maybe also go out with me." Michelle looked up at him thinking that this could be a joke but she saw the seriousness and nervousness in his eyes. She smiled and said, "Yes, Timmy I would" He kissed her head again and then said, "So, what would you like to do?" Michelle got up and took his hand and led him to the door to the house. They ran through the house and then outside running to the park. When they reached the park they slowed down and were walking now hand in hand. He took a breath and then said, "Wow, you about pulled my arm out." She laughed and then said, "Sorry, I was acting to the feeling that was inside of me and so I thought this would help" He looked at her and then said, "Huh?" She laughed again and then said, "I don't know, never mind" They laughed and then she smiled at him and he smiled back and then they started talking about anything and everything. She never felt this way about anyone and even though they had just met she knew In her heart that he was the one for her and the one that she would do anything for as well as live with for the rest of her life. She started to see that the trees were taller and the birds were happier and the grass was greener and this had never happened to her before. She also realized that what she was feeling in her chest was warm and cozy and her heart would beat faster every time she heard his voice or his soft words, than she would find herself not paying attention to anything but him. She couldn't stop thinking of him or seeing him when she wasn't with him but it happened and now that they were at the park she was trying to get closer to him but she was trying to be shy about it and so They spent every day together whether it was going to class together or him walking her home every day. Soon she realized that their relationship was growing fast and soon a couple months went by and she knew what she needed to know about him. She knew that he was the type that didn't like fights unless it was needed and he got irritated easy but not with her which she was glad. She knew that he was a strong and caring person and someone that was her best friend and hopefully more but she knew that she could tell him anything and he would not judge her. A lot of people warned her about him and said that he was a person that was dangerous but she could never see it and so she ignored them. Her parents were not sure about him and tried to give her advice about it but she knew that if her parents were here then they would think differently about him. She told them the best she could without telling them too much about his life so that they would understand, and they softer about their advice but although, everyday she got advice from them and that they wanted her to stay away from him but she never listened. She enjoyed being with him and they always went to her house and watched movies or called take out and sat at the park and talked or went to the movies and soon time flew by and they were in their next year of High School and enjoying it together with new teachers and new assignments.

Unexpected Truth. . ...

One day she was walking home with him and two guys were walking down the street toward them, she tensed as she knew them and they were guys that she dated awhile back that she forgot about. The one boy was Henry and the other was Justin and she remembered them very well because they broke up with her because she wouldn't give them what they wanted which was sex. As they walked down the street she grabbed Timmy's hand tight as they were about to pass the two boys on their left. Timmy looked at her and then saw the two boys walking toward them, Timmy didn't say anything but knew that something was going to happen because the boys were talking to each other and looking at Michelle. When they got within ear shot, Timmy heard Henry say to Justin "Man, he must not know that he isn't going to get nothing from her, because she is nothing but a nerd and isn't worth the time" Michelle looked at Timmy to see his face angry and trying to control himself. Timmy was trying to calm down but what Justin said next made him forget about calming down. Justin looked at Henry and said, "You know man maybe he does know, but who cares because she is a dull goody goody and so he might just do what he wants with her and ditch" Timmy not thinking of anything but shutting them up took a swing and hit Justin right across the mouth. Justin hit the concrete and then Henry came forward to take a swing at Timmy but Timmy backed away and Henry missed Timmy but then Timmy came back and hit Henry in the jaw sending him to the ground by his friend with blood coming from both

16

mouths. Timmy walked over and said, "If you ever talk about my girl again, I swear on my life I will kill you, you are only jealous because she wouldn't give it you but when the time is right our relationship will get to that point" He took Michelle's hand and walked her down the street leaving the boys on the road behind them. Michelle looked at him and then said, "Timmy, wow I have never had someone do that for me thank you" Timmy looked at her with soft eyes and said, "No problem Michelle they had no right talking to you like, it's your choice whether to have sex with someone or not and no one should try and force you or make you feel bad about it." She was silent for a couple of minutes and then said, "Timmy have you ever did it?" Timmy turned to her and at first he wasn't going to answer the question but then he smiled and then said, "Well, actually Michelle no I have not because I have not found the person that I want to live my life with to take it to that level." She looked at him and then said, "Oh" Timmy heard the sadness in her voice and then turned around and saw that she was feeling like he didn't want to be with her for a long time. Timmy sighed and then said, "Michelle I didn't mean it that I haven't found you yet or that I didn't want to do with you, I just meant that in general I haven't found that person, I mean I think that you are the one for me but I am not going to force you or the subject." She slowly smiled and then said, "Timmy how long have we been dating?" Timmy thought for a minute and then said, "Well, if my calculations are correct over a year" Michelle smiled and then said, "Timmy I wasn't going to tell you this yet but I feel that I need to since I have been holding it inside for the longest time." She paused and then said, "Timmy I think that I am falling in love with you" Timmy stopped and so did she and they were facing each other as cars went by on the road and then Timmy looked at her and said, "Really?" she nodded her head and then Timmy bent down and kissed her on the lips. When Timmy let go and their lips were released he looked at her and said, "I knew that I was in love with you for a while now I just never thought you felt the same way about me." She smiled and then she kissed him back and said, "Silly boy" They laughed and then walked hand in hand to her house. As they walked into her house she saw him sit down on the couch and for the first time she wanted to know and sense the feeling of touching him but she was scared and didn't know if he would go for it. She closed the door and locked it, when she walked into the living room he looked at her. Timmy saw that she was deep in thought and so he said, "Michelle what is wrong?" She didn't know what to do so she walked over and kneeled in front of him and said, "Timmy I want to take what we have to next level, if you will let me" Timmy looked confused but then he bent down and kissed her and said, "If that is what you want, but I don't want it to be because of those idiots" she laughed and said, "No, it's not because of them, I just really want to know the feel of your skin against mine and I want to feel you and know every inch of you......before she could finish Timmy had grabbed her and picked her up and carried her up the stairs. He walked to her bedroom and laid her down very gently, he took off his shirt and then she unbuttoned hers. Her body was so determined to take him now and to feel him inside of her but she knew that she wanted it to last and so she took it slow. Soon they were naked and she was crawling backwards to the pillows of the bed, as he was crawling toward her on the bed. When her head hit the pillows she relaxed and then when his body was against hers, her body was heating up faster then she had expected. He lightly touched her from her lips to her breast and then ran his finger to her belly button then further down then that and then down to her knee and then her ankle. She slowly gasped with pleasure but then as he ran his fingers back up and then inside her, she could feel the sensation and the longing and then when he released her he started to run his tongue from her chin to her breast and around each one and then move slowly down to her belly button and at this point she wanted to grab him and take him but as she waited for that moment. He slowly ran his tongue in and out of her and she couldn't help herself but to moan and then he came back up to meet her eyes and then without hesitations she pushed him down and crawled on top of him. She slowly started to kiss him from his lips to his chin and then to his neck and then slowly moved down to his bare chest and then moved slowly to his belly button running her tongue in and out of it until she knew that he was ready for her as much as she was for him. Then she slowly started to kiss past his belly button to his man hood and then slowly ran her tongue around him making him moan as well. But before she knew it she was placing him into her mouth and stroking him with every muscle and taste that she could have and as the time came closer. She finally released him and knowing that he was happy he turned her over and crawled on top of her and then was about to go further but Michelle realized that they needed to be safe. She placed her hand on Timmy's chest and said, "Timmy I want you more then you can ever imagine but unless we have protection I don't think that we should go any further" Timmy looked down at her and first she could see frustration in his eyes but then they changed to understanding. Timmy slowly moved off of her and sat on the bed, She got up and said, "Timmy what's wrong?" Timmy continued to look at the floor and ignored her question. Then he slowly got up and got dressed and then headed for the door to leave, and this made Michelle nervous and scared. She got up and grabbed her blanket that was draped over the foot of the bed. She reached him and lightly touched his arm and said, "Timmy, I do want you and this but I just think that we should be safe about it because I don't think that me getting pregnant right now would be a good thing, but I promise you that as soon as you get protection I will make up every space that was taken from today" Timmy turned around and at first she could see anger but then he said, "Michelle, I'm sorry It just took me off guard and I was so wrapped up in the moment and how much I wanted you that I didn't think about being safe but I promise that I will get some." She kissed him and then said, "Baby you don't have to go" Timmy kissed her back and then said, "Actually I do, because If I don't then I will do something that could hurt you and me and I don't want to so I am going to go but I will pick you up tomorrow for school" he turned and walked away from her leaving with sadness and the feeling of wanting to reach out and grab him and to put her arms around him and to never let him go ever. She heard the door shut and then got dressed, She made dinner and watched some TV but she knew that she would never be able to sleep knowing that she hurt him but after a couple of hours she finally fell asleep. When she woke up she quickly took a shower and then got dressed and ate her breakfast. After an hour she heard the doorbell ring and when she opened it, it was Timmy and for some reason she got this feeling that he was not himself but she couldn't put her finger on it. She knew that she shouldn't push it so she kissed him and he kissed her back. He tried to smile and then said, "Michelle I figured that maybe in a couple of days I would go to the store and get what we need and then maybe on the weekend have a couple of days to ourselves" She smiled and said, "That sounds good, I can't wait" They left that morning feeling better and as they went to school that day they knew that everything was going to be okay from now on. As Math lingered on as well as the rest of them, she couldn't stop thinking about him and wanting to be with him forever.

Fighting for Something Real. . ...

But soon she knew that they would have to fight for their relationship in which she was ready to do because she refused to lose the first person that she gave her heart too. At the end of the day Timmy was waiting for her like always, but this time she could tell by his face that something was wrong. She walked slowly to him and when she reached him she wrapped her arms around him and said, "Timmy baby what is wrong?" Timmy knowing that he could trust her but he didn't want to involve her said, "I'll tell you when we are in private" She nodded and then they walked through the halls grabbing their stuff out of the lockers and heading toward the doors to the cars by each other's side and he held out the door to her and as she got into his car she saw how tense he was and she knew that she was going to have to be calm and understanding and to be there for him as much as possible and soon he was In the driver's side and they drove to her house, but the whole time she was scared and worried for him. She knew that whatever he was going to tell her was not good. When they reached her house and entered in silence, she turned to see Timmy slowly walking to the couch and then he sat down and patted the seat near him for her to sit down next to him. She sat down and then he turned to her and said, "Michelle what I'm about to tell you is hard for me because I don't tell anyone anything that happens in my house, but since I know that I can trust you and I love you I'm going to tell you what happened last night and this morning." He paused and then said, "last night when I got home my mother

21

was lying on the floor in blood, and she had been hit by my stepfather so hard that she would not wake up." He paused again and then said, "I tried to wake her up but she wouldn't I got scared and then angry and so I walked around the house knowing that my stepfather was still home, I found him passed out drunk on his bed and the next thing I knew I slapped him for it." "He woke up and hit me so hard that I landed on the floor near the door, I was so angry that I wanted to kill him, he started calling me names and telling me how useless I was and that I will never become anything no matter how hard I tried, which made me even more angry" I tried to calm myself but then he came after me and started to swinging at me and then grabbed a baseball bat that was behind the door and then I knew that he was waiting for me, and so I grabbed the shot gun that was hidden in the closet and shot him as he was coming to me and swinging the bat at me" "I was so scared but at the same time I was so full of hate that I didn't know what to do, I ran to my mother and tried to bring her back but she was gone". I called the police and told them what happened after they came to the door, I have been sent to my real father's that lives in Atlanta, Georgia and I'm happy because my father has been trying to get me ever since I was born, but I finally found the person that I want to be with and I have to leave you. Michelle didn't know what to say or do, but she grabbed him and wrapped her arms around him and said, "Oh Timmy, I am so sorry about your mother I wish I could have made last night better for you" Timmy pulled away from her and said, "Don't you dare blame yourself, you did what you thought was right and I knew that you were" "Michelle I love you and I don't want to give myself to anyone but you, and since I don't have to leave until two weeks we will have time to make love with each other as many times." Michelle kept kissing him over and over and then he pulled back and said, "Michelle my father is coming here in a couple of days to help me and my mother's family for the funeral and all and I would like for you to be with me during it all." Michelle kissed him again and then said, "Yes, baby I will be there with you no matter what" Timmy smiled and then said, "Thank you, I love you" Michelle kissed him again and then said, "I love you too Timmy" They kissed again and then she wrapped her arms and leg around him and wouldn't let him go for anything, but then Timmy had to push her away. Michelle was hurt at first but then she said, "Timmy, If you want you can go to the store now" Timmy looked at her and then said, "I can wait Michelle" She tried to smile and then said, "But I can't Timmy, I'm going to make it up to everyday until you leave and if you won't go to the store then I will." Timmy saw the seriousness in her face and determination and then jumped up and said, "No, I'll go" she nodded and then soon he was out the door and driving down the street to the nearest store. She got up and dimmed the lights in the house and then found some fake rose pedals that she had bought for decoration for a special event and then started to spread them from the door, up the stairs, and down the hallway to her bedroom. When she stopped she grabbed the candles she had and placed a couple by the door and living room and then in her bedroom on the night side table. She took her remote to her CD player and played some soothing music. She reached into her top drawer and couldn't find anything sexy so she just got undressed and crawled into bed naked under the sheets. After 10 minutes of waiting she finally heard the door open and lock and then she heard footsteps go up the stairs and then to her bedroom that was open. When she turned her head she saw Timmy looking in and his face was priceless. He walked in and said, "Michelle you did this?" she smiled and said, "Yes, I did, now come here and let me show you my magic" She didn't have to wait long before he was naked and next to her in the bed. She slowly got on top of him and began to slowly run her tongue from his chin to his chest and then around each nipple and then she moved to his belly button and once there she passionately kissed him on his sides and then moved down to the part of him that she wanted and then slowly took him and caressed every inch of him until he moaned out of pleasure that was so wild that she knew that he was ready. She slowly got off him and soon he was on top of her making sure that the pleasure was returned and she could feel him hands running and touching her body with every motion and every feeling and nerve of his fingers. She moaned out of pleasure and then soon he ran his fingers inside of her and made her ready for him even more then before but before she knew it he had stopped and then his tongue was playing with her and running in and out of her and soon she was moaning louder than anyone could have heard from her. He released her and then crawled on top of her and soon he slowly inserted himself inside of her and within that moment she could feel all of him. She could feel his pain, his love for her, his fears, his sadness, everything that he held inside she could see and feel herself. She realized that this was part of her gift but she didn't want it to ruin everything so she moved with him and enjoyed every minute of it as they were together as one. It lasted as long as she had hoped and when they were done, they were so sore that they fell to the bed in sweat and exhaustion. But as she looked at him she knew that she loved him and that she wanted more. Timmy looked at her smiled and then said, "How was it?" She laughed and then moved upward so that she could be right near him face to face and then she kissed him and said, "Timmy that was amazing" Timmy smiled and said, "Yes it was, you were awesome" they laughed and then saw that the sheets needed to be changed badly. Timmy jumped up and said, "Michelle are you okay? I didn't hurt you did I?" Michelle looked at him and then said, "NO Timmy you didn't this is normal for a girl that has never had sex before." He was confused and thought that she was trying to make him feel better but then she said, "Timmy I gave myself to you like you did to me" Timmy looked at her and said, "I know and I'm happy you did, it's just that it is a lot of blood and I just wanted to make sure that you are okay" She smiled and then said, "I'm okay" he said, "Okay, well why don't you go into the bathroom and clean up and I'll fix the sheets" She nodded and grabbed her clothes then moved to the bathroom, when she got inside the bathroom she was happy but not sure how long the bleeding would take. She closed the bathroom door and then grabbed a pad from the cabinet and then cleaned herself the best she could and then put her clothes on with the pad in place and then walked out the bathroom back to her room. When she got there Timmy was done putting new sheets on the bed and then the comforter. She walked over to the other side of her bed and lay down next to Timmy who had also gotten dressed while she was in the bathroom. Timmy had put on her TV and so they watched as many shows as they could and never moved until she looked at Timmy and said, "Baby, are you hungry?" Timmy looked down at her and said, "Actually, I am what can we eat?" She jumped up and walked toward the door and said, "I'll surprise you" When she left she saw him smile and it made her smile as well. She went down into the kitchen and realized that it was around 4:30pm so she cooked a early dinner for them and she made chicken and rice and green beans, after about an hour or so she took the chicken out of the oven and turned off the stove and then she made his and hers and then took the plates upstairs with cokes in her hands and when she reached the bedroom, he looked at her and said, "Oh, baby I was wondering why you were gone so long, you didn't have to do that" She smiled and said, "Yes, I did" He took his plate and sat up in her bed and started to eat as well as she did sitting next to him. When they were finished he took his plate and hers downstairs and put them into the sink. As he headed back upstairs and peeked through the door of her bedroom, he saw her peacefully lying down with her eyes closed and she was sleeping. He walked in and when she didn't move he had a flash back of his mother, he didn't know what to do but Michelle heard him breathing hard and it woke her up. She looked at him and saw the horror on his face, she jumped up and grabbed him and wrapped her arms around him. She kissed him and said, "What's wrong?" He snapped back to reality and said, "I'm sorry, I came back and you were sleeping and when I hit the door by accident and you didn't move, it brought back flash backs of my mother" She grabbed him tighter and pulled him back to the bed where they were laying and when they hit the pillows, she never let go of him. She wrapped her arms around him as he faced her and said, "Timmy, I'm sorry honey but I am okay and your mom is safe now, I'm here for you and so lay with me and I'll take away the pain as much as I could." Timmy buried closer to her and they kissed each other and soon she was trying to see if her gift would let her take away his pain and so she reached into his mind with her thoughts and found a way to make him feel better and soon he was relaxed and happy again and the pain was a small part of him now. She kissed his forehead and then his lips and then watched him sleep for a couple of minutes before she slowly drifted to sleep herself. She knew that soon he would have to leave her but for now she was going to make sure that she spent as much time with as she could.

A Hidden Emotion comes true. . ..

As the sun shined into the bedroom and hit the wall, Michelle slowly opened her eyes and reached over to the side of her bed where Timmy was sleeping to find that it was empty and she felt alone and sad knowing that he must have left in the middle of the night. She sat up and draped her legs to the floor and walked down stairs to the smell of eggs and bacon and coffee. When she reached the kitchen she saw Timmy cooking his heart out and she smiled as she watched him cooking. When she got to the bar counter that was a part of the kitchen and Timmy looked up and smiled and said, "Good Morning darling, I thought that I would make you breakfast before we started our day of school" She smiled and took the coffee cup that he handed her and she looked at the clock and saw that it was 5:30am and they had time to eat and take showers before they would have to go to school. So, she sat down at the table that was in the kitchen across of him as he sat down and handed her plate and put his in front of him. She watched him for a couple of minutes and when he looked up from his plate and he said, "What is it Michelle?" She smiled and said, "I thought that you left me last night when I woke up and saw that you were not there, but I'm glad that you stayed" He smiled and said, "Why would I leave you without saying anything, last night was not a one night thing silly, but I'm sorry I should have said something to you" She smiled and said, "No, it's okay, I'm just glad that you are still here and it felt good coming down the stairs seeing the man that I love cooking for me" They both laughed and then finished their breakfast. Timmy took her plate and his and placed it into the sink and then turned around and said, "You know Michelle we still have time for some fun so I'll race you to the bathroom" Michelle laughed out loud and then realized that he was being serious and took off from the table and ran up the stairs toward her bathroom and giggled as she saw Timmy running after her saying that he was going to get her and tickle her until she can't breathe. When she reached the door of her bathroom she almost fell but Timmy caught her and slowly walked with her into the bathroom. Without hesitations they striped their clothes off and joined each other into the hot water that was steaming over the curtains and when the water hit them their bodies relaxed and soon he was scrubbing her body with her body wash and she was scrubbing his with his body wash. He washed her hair as she did his as every muscle of their bodies was wanting more. When they finished rinsing off, Michelle kissed him under the hot water and soon Timmy lifted her up and her legs went around his body as he slowly went inside of her and as the water hit them with every moment and feeling relaxing them and making it even better. They were once again making love and it lasted even longer than before. When they finished they turned off the water and took their towels and dried off as they were walking out of the bathroom. She pulled her clothes out of her drawers as he pulled his out of his duffle bag and then after they were dressed, they grabbed their book bags and headed for the door to go to school. They got into the car and she got this feeling that today was going to be an interesting day, but she smiled as they arrived to school. They were early but she didn't care, they walked inside and sat down with their friends and waited for the bell to ring. After an hour of talking with friends and chatting about the assignments due the bell rang and they got up and Timmy walked her to her first class which was Math. He kissed her and said, "I'll be waiting for you after class, I love you" She smiled and kissed him back and then said, "I can't wait" She watched him walk away in the direction of his class and then sat down in her seat waiting for the teacher to start and so that the class would end so she could be with her Timmy again. The teachers went on about fractions and graphs that were more complicated then she had ever seen but she understood it and worked on her problems in a short time as well as her homework so that she could have free time. The bell rang for class to be over, she jumped up and grabbed her stuff and headed for the door. When she opened it she saw Timmy waiting for her like always. He smiled at her and then took her hand, they walked to the next class and it was English then next was Science, Computer, History, Spanish, and then last was P.E. and when the bell rang for school to end. Everyone exited like as if it was summer and Michelle found herself searching for Timmy since his class was further away and she knew that he would be looking for her on the terrace. She was looking everywhere but didn't see him, she felt sad and thought that something had happened and so she sat down on the concrete railing and before she knew it, she saw a boy that had liked her a year ago coming in her direction. She tensed up and was trying to act like she was busy, but it didn't work. He came over and sat down next to her. His name was Jack but she never knew his last name because she didn't care nor did she know anything about him just that he gave her the creeps and that he was obsessed with her, she looked at him and said, "Can I help you?" He smiled at her and said, "Why so rude?" She was disgusted and said, "What do you want Jack?" He laughed and said, "Oh, right you're waiting on your boyfriend, well, I saw him talking to that sexy girl oh what's her name oh yeah Veronica right, he was talking to her and smiling." Michelle was not normally the one to get jealous or mad at that kind of thing but something inside of her wanted to rip Jack's head off but she sat still and said, "Jack, I know why he's talking to her, he's tutoring her and he's allowed to have other friends besides me, plus, if he was going to be with someone else then he would tell me and it's not your business but ours." Michelle suddenly felt really angry and then she said, "Jack I know that you still have feelings for me, but I never liked you and you can try and break me and Timmy up all you want to but it won't work because I love him and you will never get your chance." She stood up leaving him with his anger and rage and as she stood up Timmy was standing there watching her. She looked at him and then at Jack, then she knew that he heard what they said to each other but she saw that he was mad at jack and not her, and she was glad about. Timmy walked over to her put his arm around her waist and then bent her backwards in front of Jack and kissed her hard and passionately. When he brought her back up they could see that Jack was about to explode with anger. They laughed and then Timmy looked right at jack and said, "First of all, Veronica is just a friend and I am helping her with math, second I would never cheat or hurt Michelle and third it is none of your business about our relationship and you will never have her because I'm going to marry her and you will never have that chance." Michelle was shocked and Jack was even angrier, but Timmy took her hand and they ran down the stairs to the parking lot and then when they got into his car, Michelle looked at him and said, "Timmy is that true?" Timmy smiled and said, "Michelle you know how I feel about you, and I would like to marry you and I'm hoping that we can someday" Michelle felt happy and sad at the same time because that would mean that they would have to find each other because he was leaving at the end of the week to go with his father to Atlanta, Georgia. Timmy saw the sadness in her eyes and then placed his hand on her leg and said, "It will be okay Michelle, I promise that I will find you and soon I will be old enough to be on my own and I will find you." She smiled and said, "Same here Timmy" They kissed and then he started up his Ford mustang and they drove out to the streets and headed to her house. She never asked to go to his because she knew that was hard for him, but she knew that he had told his father that he was going to stay with her. She never expected his father to find her parents and ask if it was okay, but after his father had explained what had happened to his mother to them her parents were okay with it and realized that he was not so bad and so they have been supporting her decision to be with him and helping them as much as possible. Her father called her the night before and told her and that if she needed anything he would give it to her, but she told him that they were okay and then they told her that they probably wouldn't be able to come home until a couple weeks instead of this week. She knew that they were busy but she was glad because this gave her the time with Timmy that she needed, she remembered this as they drove to her house. When she came back to the present, Timmy was holding her door open and helping her out of the car and soon they were heading to the front door. As they walked into her house she felt this happy and peaceful feeling that everything was going to be okay. Even though it was Wednesday and he was leaving on Monday she knew that one day destiny would bring them back together. She just hoped that they would keep in touch and that their life's would not make them go separate ways, meaning that he wouldn't find someone else but she knew that she can't control that. She did know that she would never love anyone else, she knew that was harsh but she wouldn't let her heart be hurt again and so she decided that after he left she would close her heart out to everyone that caused her pain and that wanted to be with her. She snapped back to reality and found Timmy looking at her, she laughed and said, "Sorry, I was day dreaming" He kept looking at her and then said, "Michelle, I don't know I just saw but it felt like you were fighting with yourself almost". She laughed out loud and then said, "I had an image that you feel in love with someone else and so I was planning in my head that it would not happen to me." Timmy grabbed her and said, "I could never love anyone else but you and you know that." Michelle buried her head into his shoulder and then said, "I know but sometimes it happens and you can't control it and I will never get mad at you if you do, just know that I will always love you and will always be here for you." Timmy hugged her tighter and said, "I will always love you and be here for you no matter what and you have my heart and no one will ever have it but you" Michelle kissed him on the neck and then his lips and then said, "You have my heart as well and it will only belong to you for the rest of my days alive." She pulled away and looked at him and saw that he was sad and knew that leaving was going to hurt them both, but she smiled and said, "It's going to be okay baby so now we will watch TV and lay on the couch until dinner time." Timmy agreed to this and then they walked to the couch and he sat down in the middle and then she laid down placing her head in his lap as he played with her hair and she turned the channels of the TV and finally they found a good action movie and for awhile their troubles and worries were gone. When she woke up the next morning it was Thursday and the day was shining bright but her heart felt like each day would make her tare even deeper as the thought of him leaving would come to life. She slowly got up and saw that Timmy was a sleep sitting up on the couch like the movie was still playing and she realized that she fell asleep with her head still on his lap. She looked at the clock and it was 5:30 am and they still had about an hour or so before school. She got up and leaned in next to Timmy and then kissed him slowly, when she pulled away he slowly opened his eyes and smiled. She smiled back and then he kissed her back. She got up and went to the kitchen to fix them something quick and decided to make pancakes and coffee. Timmy slowly walked behind her while she was making the pancakes and wrapped his arms around her waist and then kissed her neck. She moved her face into his and kissed him back. He let her go and then went to help and make some coffee, she turned around and said, "Timmy if want to you can go ahead and take a shower and then after we eat I will take one and then we can head off to school." Timmy smiled and then said, "I'll wait for you my love, I am in no hurry" She giggled and then said, "Okay" After 10 minutes or so everything was ready and they were sitting down and eating and drinking their coffee. When they finished and their plates were in the sink, they headed up to the bathroom and joined each other into the shower again like the morning before and this time the experience was more exciting and loving then before. After their shower they got dressed and grabbed their stuff for school and headed out the door to his Mustang. When they got to the car, he blasted his heavy metal and then started to the car and headed to school like nothing will change or nothing had changed except that he had the woman of his heart and dreams. He felt alive and that everything was going to be okay. When they got to school, everything was the same except that they were told that they were going to have Friday and the weekend off from school. Everyone was excited, but Michelle knew that those days were going to be her last and that his dad would be here Sunday night to take him away from her.

The Hurt that never goes away. . . . . .

She dealt with the pain that hit her heart but kept going on with school, than when the bell rang for 3pm for them to be released she knew that she had to spend her time wisely with Timmy before he left for good. When she saw Timmy waiting for her, she knew in her heart that she could never love anyone so much and that she would be badly hurt when he left. But she forced a smile and walked over to him like nothing was wrong. He looked at her knowing that he saw the pain in her body language and her eyes, but he swore to himself that he would never love anyone as much as she and that he would do everything in his power to make it work. He took her hand when she reached him and then they walked to his mustang that was in the same spot as always. When they left the parking lot, an old fast car drove by fast and almost hit another car trying to pull out and with this she said out loud, "Idiot". Timmy laughed and said, "No Kidding" but then when she saw the boy driving she could feel his pain and why he was in a hurry. She relaxed her thoughts and said to the boy, "It will be okay and workout" She saw the boy look at her and then he smiled and she found herself smile too. After he was gone and out of site, she stopped smiling worrying if Timmy saw the connection but he was driving and not paying attention. She felt like she had seen the boy before but it didn't matter now, they were out of the traffic and on their way to her house. As they were driving he passed her street and so she turned to Timmy and said, "Where are we going?" Timmy turned to her and said, "I thought that today we would hang out outside of the house and do some stuff if you wanted too "She smiled and said, "Sure" Timmy reached over and kissed her as he pulled to a stop at the stop light, and then she said, What you would like to do?" When the green light came he kept his eyes on the road, but said, "Anything that you want, you pick" So, she sat in silent thinking of what they could do. She pulled out her digital camera and then said, "We should take pictures together, like at the beach, or the park, and at the house in the yard or something." He smiled even bigger and said, "That is a great idea, then we can get them developed and then maybe go to a movie and dinner and then when we get home we can separate them and put them photo albums so that we will have them forever" She smiled at this thought and then said, "Exactly" Timmy drove to the beach and since it was packed at that time of day, they walked along the beach and took some pictures together and some with just her and just him. After a couple of hours, they left and then headed to the park and took a couple there and then went back to her house and found that her swing in the back was the perfect place for them for pictures and so they took some there and some by the pool. When they were finished with the pictures they had around 100 with different poses and they were all good. She saved them to the memory card and then took it out and they went to Wal-Mart and waited an hour for them to get developed and went shopping until then. After they paid for everything and took everything to the car, Timmy walked in and picked up the photos. After 10 minutes later he left Wal-Mart and got into the car, giving them to her and then when she held them for a couple of minutes she looked through them and then as he drove off. Timmy turned to her and said, "Well, how did they come out?" She smiled at him and said, "Oh, Timmy they came out wonderful" He laughed and said, "Good" Then he pulled out to the highway and then said, "Well, should we eat first or movie first?" She looked at the clock and it read 6:30pm and the movie didn't start until 8:00pm. She turned to Timmy and said; "Let's eat first since we have time" He nodded and said, "Okay where would you like to go then My Michelle?" She smiled at this and then said, "Well, somewhere quick but good priced, so I would say Bojangles" He smiled and then said, "I was just thinking that" They laughed and they pulled into the drive-thru of the restaurant and ordered through the speaker. After they paid and got their food, they drove off and pulled into the small movie theater and ate their food with the music going. When they were finished they threw away their trash and then Timmy and Michelle walked to the window and he bought the tickets for them. They made good time because the movie didn't start for an hour so they walked into the theater and went to the bathroom. When they came back after washing their hands, they walked over to the counter and Timmy got popcorn to share and a large drink. Michelle told him that she didn't want anything else because she was full. They grabbed their stuff and napkins and straws and headed to their movie. They found seats in the back and sat down waiting for the movie to start as everyone started to pile in from nowhere. She rested her head on his shoulder and he kissed her forehead, and after awhile of waiting the lights went dark and soon the commercials came on. She could hear and see many people talking but she just kept close to Timmy, and soon the movie started and it was more intense but good then what she thought. It was about a girl who fell in love and her parents and didn't understand and then he got killed and through the movie she spent her life trying to solve his case until the day she died. Which she did and in the movie she was in her thirties when she found out the truth about why he was killed and how he was killed and then she went after the guy herself after training for it and being able to defend herself and kill the guy herself. She died happy and at peace knowing that she did what she had to make it right and to give him and his family justice. Michelle could relate to this in some form, but Timmy kissed her and took her hand to take her outside and then she realized that she was so wrapped up into the movie that she didn't know that it ended. They exited and entered his car which was warm and cozy; they talked about the movie the whole way home. When they got home it was about 11:00pm and then they pulled out their photo albums that they had bought at Wal-Mart and started to separate the doubles of the pictures and put them in each one so that they could both have one. It took them an hour or so and then they left them on the table and headed to her room to go to sleep.

She knew that Tomorrow was going to be Friday and that she was going to only have a couple days and she would fear Sunday when his father came and took him away from her forever, but she relaxed as she slept and let everything go as far as her emotions and her fears. She dreamt of them sitting on the beach in the middle of summer a couple years down the road and in the dream she was In a white dress and he was in a tuxedo and all of their family and friends were there and soon she realized that it was the happiest day of her life and that she was no longer Ms. Hallmar but Mrs. Oxford and she knew in this dream that everything was going to be okay. When she woke up the next morning, Timmy was wrapped around her and she buried her head deeper into his chest as he slept and then she kissed him on the lips not moving as she cuddled closer to him. He never moved and she just laid there staring at the ceiling thinking of everything that they could do to keep it together and see each other and nothing seem right or seemed to be able to work out. She stared at the ceiling for a long time and didn't realize that Timmy had woken up and was starring at her. She finally had this feeling that he was looking at her and she turned to him and smiled. Timmy kept looking at her and then he said, "Are you okay, My Michelle I have been watching you for the past 30 minutes and you never moved your eyes from the ceiling and for a minute it scared me" She locked eyes with him and then said, "I was trying to find ways for us to be together while we were far away from each other and nothing seems to be right or a chance of working out" Timmy hugged her close and held her for a while before releasing her. He looked at her and said, "I have one that might work?" She looked at him excited and then unsure. He said, "Well, you can come with me?" She smiled at the thought and then said, "Timmy I can't go with you, there is something about me that you don't and the reason why I haven't told you is because I don't know myself but I do know that it is something that I will have to figure out and solve myself." Then she said, "I wish I could come with you, I love you with all of my heart and I want to be your wife so bad that I can see it in my dreams and my heart but I think that it would be hard right now" She saw the disappointment in his eyes and then she said, "how about this, we can either be together and then after graduation, I can fly to you or you fly to me or we can pause us for now and then see what happens after graduation and go from there" Timmy was quite for a minute and then said, "well, I will go with the first choice then." She smiled and then said, "Me too" They smiled at each other and then Timmy said, "Great now we don't have to worry about it until then" She nodded and then said, "What would like to do today?" but even though she wanted that to be true she didn't know what a couple of years would bring or what would happen at that time so she tried to be strong and act like nothing was wrong and so she smiled at him and then listened and watched as Timmy smiled and then said, "You" Michelle giggled as he moved on top of her and started kissing her and tickling her and she couldn't stop laughing and then he stopped and kissed so firmly and passionately that her body sent a heat wave through her and once again she wanted him so bad that she couldn't take it. She looked up at Timmy and whispered in his ear, "Timmy, take me" He smiled and said, "My Pleasure my love" and before she knew it they were one again and it was wonderful. She laid there afterwards thinking of their life together and then for some reason she came back to reality and cuddled closer to Timmy who was watching TV. They laid there for the longest time watching TV together and then she called take out for lunch because they had skipped breakfast and when the delivery man came with the food and rang the door bell, Timmy got up and dressed and walked downstairs to get it for them. They ate in bed and then finished watching TV and then moved on to movies. Before she knew it was dark outside and it was time for dinner and so they got dressed and walked downstairs and cooked dinner together. They sat down on the couch waiting for it to be done; while they watched TV she had an idea. She turned to Timmy and said, "I was wondering, do you want to rent some movies tonight and just chill and eat dinner here and watch movies all night?" He looked at her and then said, "I think that is a great idea" Then he said, "I'll go get them, what kind would you like?" She smiled and said, "It doesn't matter I trust you" He smiled and said, "Okay, I will be right back, I love you" Michelle kissed him and said, "I love you too" As soon as he left the timer said 20 minutes which was plenty of time and so she didn't move from the couch but kept watching TV and waited for him to come back.

A Vision . . ..

After awhile she had drifted off into a dark place in her mind and it was all black around her and soon she saw this boy that was in trouble and she realized that it was the boy that she had seen at the school. She looked further and saw that he was getting beat up for something that had to do with his past and she thought to herself but trying to help him that the boys that were hurting this kid would feel the pain that they were placing on him until they died. And soon the boy was freed and leaning against the wall thanking her in his thoughts. She didn't know if the boy knew it was her or not but she had to do something, the boys died out of nowhere and then the kid ran as hard as he could and vanished into the night. Once he was safe she came back to her living room, and then saw that the timer was going off and when she turned from the couch to check the food she saw Timmy standing by the couch holding the movies in his hand. She stopped and said, "Oh, Timmy I didn't know that you were back yet" Timmy just starred at her and watched her move to the kitchen and pulled dinner out and served them on plates for them. Timmy walked over to her and said, "What was that?" She looked up at him and said, "What?" Timmy looked at her and said, "You were talking to the air, and saying that you wanted three boys to die from the pain that they were inflicting on another boy and then you said you were welcome and then I saw life come back into your eyes." She didn't know what to say or how to explain it. She took a deep breath and said, "Timmy I see when people are in trouble and I can save them or kill them by my words or thoughts, and while you were gone I had a vision of this kid getting beat up and I had to help him." Timmy looked at her and then realized that she was not lying to him, which he never thought she would it seemed kind of strange and not normal. But he said, "What else can you do?" She looked at him and said, "I don't know it hasn't progressed right now that is it" Timmy walked over to her and said, "Well, you don't have to be afraid and you could have told me, I would have rather been prepared for it instead of being scared out of mind" She looked at him and smiled and said, "Sorry, I didn't want to worry you or make you think that I was crazy" Timmy laughed and said, "Trust me Baby, I already think that you are crazy in love with me like I am you and If you have this gift then we will do it together." She smiled and then reached over and kissed him. He kissed her back and then they took their plates over to the couch and ate dinner on the couch next to each other and watched the first movie that he had chosen. After the first movie was done about an hour and half he turned to her and said, "Can I ask you a question?" She looked at him and saw in his face that he was curious and so she said, "I will tell you what I know" He nodded in understanding and then said, "When does it happen?" She smiled and then said, "It only happens when someone is in trouble or needs my help or advice or if I go looking for someone that needs me which I can feel. But it happens very often but not to the point where I can't think or function. Most of the time it happens when I am by myself and not at school, or at work or anywhere around people." He nodded and said, "Oh, Okay" She looked at him and then said, "Are you going to ask me, why this happens?" He said, "I was going to but part of me doesn't want to know" She frowned at this and then said, "Well, it's good that you didn't ask me because I don't why this happens to me but I intend to figure out but I do know that whatever this is will be with me for the rest of my life and it will never go away." He watched her as she spoke and then when she was finished he said, "Well, then I will be by your side forever and nothing will change that and I'm sorry if I hurt you, this is just a lot for me to take in but I am with you all the way." She smiled and said, "Thank you, that makes me feel better, I love you Timmy and I know that this is hard for you but it is what I was given and I have to do my best with it and live with it." Timmy nodded and then kissed her and then he got up and put in the second movie and cuddled closer to her. They watched the movie in silence and when it was done and over, she looked at the clock and it read 10:00pm. She turned to Timmy and realized that he had fallen asleep and so she turned off the TV and took the movie out and laid back down against him and closed her eyes as she fell asleep with him and he hugged her closer to him. She dreamed peacefully that night but then when she woke up the next morning everything came back to her and she realized that her happiness was going to end. When she opened her eyes she saw that Timmy had turned on the TV and was waiting for her wake up. She got up and looked at him and he looked down at her, she smiled at him and then saw in his expression that he wanted to say something to her. She sat up and said, "What is it?" Timmy sighed and then said, "I just got a phone call from my father and he told me that he would be here by tonight, and that we would be leaving Sunday afternoon at around 4 at the latest." He sighed again and then said, "Me and him are driving to Atlanta Georgia and when we get there I start school on Monday at the Booker T. Washington High School and then on the weekends I have to get a job somewhere." Michelle stayed silent and then when she realized that he was finished she said, "Timmy, I hope that we can stay in touch because I am going to go crazy without you here" Timmy looked down at her and first he just looked at her and didn't say anything. Then he said, "Me too babe, me too" He leaned down and kissed her and then said, "Well, I am going to go and make sure that I have everything packed and since I am not going back to that house to get everything else which I should, never mind I think I will go get everything else from there I need the time to think and then I will come back and then we will do whatever you want to do okay." She looked at him as she saw that he was really taking this hard, and then said, "Okay" He got up and went upstairs and she heard the door close, and for the first time in her life she grabbed the pillow next to her and buried her face into it and she thought she had her emotions under control but then she let out a scream into the pillow and then started to cry and soon she was crying so hard that she got up from the couch and step outside so that he could not hear her. She looked up at the sky and saw that it was beautiful and full of life and yet she felt full of pain and anger, and wished that she could leave everything and go with him but she couldn't. She sat on the steps of the deck and put her hands into her face and started crying again until she couldn't anymore. She got up and walked back into the house, when she closed the door she stopped and tried to control herself. She walked upstairs and opened her door to find him putting his clothes and things into the bag and then she sat on the bed. Timmy turned to her hearing her sitting down and then when he saw her face, he raced over and said, "What's wrong?" She tried to breath and get her breathe and then she said, "Timmy, I have to be honest with you, I have never cried before now and I hate it, also, I feel as if the world has pulled the rug underneath me." Timmy pulled her close and was silent for a few moments and then he said, "I feel the same way, I have never wanted to be with someone as much as I do you and I have never loved anyone as much as you." Then he said, "I am torn so bad that I am tempted to tell my father to leave me here so that I can be with you but I know that I can't." She started to cry even harder and then he hugged her close and kissed the top of her head and then her tears and then he lips. He looked into her eyes and said, "Michelle, I promise on my life that after high school I will come for you and then we will be together forever if you still would do me the honor of being my beloved wife." Michelle smiled at this and then said, "Yes, Timmy Yes" He smiled and then said, "God, I love you" She kissed him and said, "I love you too" He let her go and then moved back across the room to finish packing and then while she waited and watched him, she saw every moment and motion and language in his body and soon she couldn't take her eyes off him. But she knew that this was the last time she was going to see him and so she said, "Timmy, All I want to do tonight is spend it with you and order food for here and make love to you until we can't anymore." Timmy turned his head in her direction and then said, "Sounds good to me love" He turned back and finished packing everything and then turned around and said, "Well, since it is morning I will go get breakfast for us, but first I will go get the rest of my stuff from the house." She nodded and then watched him walk out the door. He turned around when he got to the door and came back to her and said, "I will be right back baby, I love you" Then he kissed her and she said, "I love you too" He disappeared around the corner and when she heard the front door close she could feel the tears rolling down her face but she tried to push them back but it didn't work. And soon she was grabbing her pillows and crying into them. She couldn't stop but after awhile, she slowly calmed down and laid there and slowly drifted off to sleep from crying so much. When she woke up almost two hours later she saw Timmy sitting by her trying to wake her up. She looked at him and said, "Sorry, I must have fallen asleep." He looked at her and said, "You did, but you were also having a very vivid dream that was scaring me" She looked at him and said, "What kind?" He looked at the floor and then said, "It sounded like you were having a dream or vision of me and you falling in love with other people and never talking after I left" She looked at him and said, "Promise me that it won't happen" he looked down at the floor and said, "Michelle I don't know what is going to happen all I know is that I love you and will fight to be with you and will do everything in my power to make sure that we are together in the end." She sighed and said, "Same here" he kissed her and then took her hand and led her downstairs to eat what he had brought back from a diner.

Believed Words of the Heart. . . . .

They ate in silence and then she took their plates and put them in the sink and then turned to him and watched his body relax while he drank his coffee and then said, "Timmy, I want you" He slowly put down his cup and stood up from the table and then the next thing she knew he was holding her against the counter and he said, "Where?" She said, "Anywhere" He smiled and said, "Your wish be done" She giggled at this thought and then he pinned her against the counter and then pulled her thighs up and soon she was wrapped around him and she was sitting on the counter. Her body was filled with power and excitement that everything that was happening was a blur and fast passed and soon she felt like everything went dark, but she kept her eyes on him and soon everything made sense and she was happy and full of love and passion. When they were done and they released each other, he kissed her firm and harder than before and then leaned against her, then he wrapped his arms around her with his naked body and said into her ears, "Michelle, I love you with all of my heart and soul and we are not finished yet" She smiled at him when he pulled his face away and said, "I can't wait" She kissed him and then they put on their clothes and walked over to the living room to watch the movies they had rented from the night before. Soon, it was lunch time and so they went out to lunch and then took a stroll in the park and around the beach. When they got home they were tired but still full of energy and so they realized that it would not too long before he would get a call from his dad and then they wouldn't be a lone and so they took the time they had to make love to each other until they couldn't or until they had no more energy. After hours of energy and love being passed and expressed to each other, they called take out and then waited for his father. Timmy got the food from the delivery guy when the door bell rang and then fixed hers and his and they ate and watched TV. After they were finished with their meals, Timmy's phone went off. Timmy reached for it and saw that it was his father, he said, "Hello" then listened. Timmy got up and went to the door. When he opened it, he was happy but sad at the same time. Timmy's dad walked through the door holding a bag that was just for the night and then he turned to Michelle and said, "Hi, Michelle I am Henry Oxford, I know that this is hard for you and Timmy but I have no choice but to do this and I have been fighting for him since his mother left me. " "But I do understand that you love each other, and you are welcome to come with us or to visit anytime you want too." She smiled and said, "Thank you and it is nice to meet you" He smiled back and said, "You too honey." He put his bag on the floor and then said, "You have a lovely home here, and By the way where can I sleep?" Michelle got up and said, "I can show you, this way." She moved up the stairs and then opened a door that was the quest room and he walked in and put his bag on the bed. He turned to her and said, "Thank you, I think I will take a shower if that is okay and then we can either talk or go out or something." Michelle smiled and then said, "Well, we just ate but we can get you something" He nodded and then said, "I can cook that will be fine with me" Then he said, "I will be done shortly" She nodded and then closed the door and then went back downstairs and wrapped her arms around Timmy as he kissed her over and over. They went back to the TV and waited for his father to come down. He arrived about 15 minutes later and then looked around in the kitchen and found some chicken and rice and green beans and then started cooking. After he was finished and it was all done he fixed his plate and joined them on the big couch. He ate his dinner and watched the TV show that they were sucked into which was CSI and then after he was done, he got up and then put his dish in the sink and put the food away. When he came back he said to the kids "Is there anything that you guys want to do tonight?" Michelle looked at Timmy and Timmy looked at her and then Timmy said, "We could go for a walk on the beach or see a movie" Michelle smiled and said, "That sounds nice" His dad smiled and said, "Yes, it does, okay lets go" So, they walked out the door 5 minutes later and Michelle locked the door behind them. They got into Timmy's dad's Chevy Malibu and then drove off to the beach and it was a good night because it was warm but there was a breeze. They walked farther than they had ever imagined talking about everything and planning after graduation and then when they came back to their car, they were tired. But they got in and then drove to the theaters and got popcorn, candy, and soda. They agreed on an action movie and then watched in with a full theater and while the movie played all she could think of were Timmy and she getting married. As this thought came to mind she couldn't help but smile, Timmy held her hand and then leaned in and kissed her on the lips. They turned back to the movie and watched it until it was over. When they got out of the movies, they knew that it was time to call it a night and so they went back to her house and her and Timmy went to her bedroom and crashed quickly while his father did the same in the other bedroom. When they woke up, they made breakfast and took showers and got ready. The next thing she knew Timmy and his father were packing up the car and getting ready to leave. She was fighting back tears the whole time and as she watched him move slow and from the car into the house she wanted to pack her stuff and go with him but she also knew that she couldn't do it. So, she stood there in silence and as the time had come to an end she saw him stop in front of her and grabbed her close and would not stop kissing her and before she knew it tears were falling like a waterfall and she couldn't talk and Timmy slowly whipped them from her eyes and said, "I love you my darling" She tried to smile but the tears wouldn't stop and then she said choking on them, "I love you my Timmy" He kissed her one more time and then headed for the door and she knew that after this point he would be gone forever. She yelled, "Wait" and when he turned she ran up the stairs and grabbed a necklace that she had since forever and it had a picture of her in it and was locked in a locket in the shape of a heart. She darted back downstairs and put it on him and said, "I want you to have this so that you will never forget me and our love" He looked down at it and then back at her and said, "Darling, I could never forget you or our love" Then he pulled something out of his bag and it was a necklace as well except more manly and it was gold and like a chain and he put it around her neck and then kissed her. He walked away and shut the door behind him. She ran to the window and watched him get in the car and put him head into his hands as his father drove off. She knew that from that day on her life was going to change and that she would never be able to give her heart to anyone. She stood there an awhile trying to wrap her head around everything that had happened and since she didn't know who to run to for advice she just went to her bedroom and shut the door. She fell on her bed and before she knew it she couldn't stop crying and then after awhile she fell into a deep sleep. When she woke up she checked her cell that was on her table that was next to her bed and saw that he had called her like 5 times. She dialed the number back and when she heard his voice she started crying again. He tried to calm her down but it didn't work, but after awhile she was able to talk to him for awhile before he got off and told her that he would call her when he got there. She went back to sleep after eating something and when she woke up it was time for school. She slowly got ready and drove to school this time, thinking that it would help but it didn't and the whole day felt like an empty hole and when it was over she went home not sure what to do to get her mind and body back to normal. She looked at her phone and saw that he hadn't called her. She did her homework and then went on the computer for a little bit and then watched TV but even that didn't help because she could still feel his presence and know that he would be coming around the corner to her. She only found that he wasn't there, and soon she didn't realize how fast time went by. Before she knew it a month went by and he had never called her and she knew that he was there already but she didn't want to call him because she knew that she would be upset and start crying again. One night she was sitting on the couch and watching TV and suddenly everything went black and everything disappeared and soon she could see Timmy at school and then home and in the vision he was talking to this girl and he called her Shelly Barns and he was kissing her and holding her. In the vision he was happy but she could feel that his heart still belonged to her and that he didn't love this girl as much as her which made her happy but at the same time sad. She also saw that he was trying to get on with his life and it felt like he had forgotten about their arrangement after graduation and so this made her heart start to crumble and burn and soon the vision started to disappear and when she came back to reality she couldn't fight back the tears. She grabbed her phone and dialed his number and when he picked up all she could say was "How could you?" She heard the other side of the phone be silent and then he said, "I'm sorry my dear I didn't plan it, it just happened and I don't love her like you trust me I want to be with you forever but she was there for me and I tried to call you but every time I tried to pick up the phone I knew that if I heard your voice or your tears that it would just make it harder for both of us." She spoke strong and firm and it shocked him and she said, 'Well, then I guess you don't have to worry about me anymore, I hope you are happy with her and live a happy life together." Before she hung up she heard him say, "Wait, darling you don't understand I don't want her, I want you always." Then she said, "Then show it and by you kissing her and loving her and giving your heart to her is not helping." He got silent and then said, "Your right, and I'm sorry, I just don't know what to do and how I can deal with it" She sighed and then said, "I'm sorry I shouldn't do this to you, if you want to be with her that is your choice not mine, I'm not going to stop you." He sighed and said, "No, you're right I'm not making this easy on both of us and I don't want her I want you so I promise that I will fight to be with you and do what I can so that I can come to you and marry you when we are free of school" Then he said, "I have to go babe, my dad wants me to cook tonight, I love you and I will call you soon" She couldn't say anything but "I love you too". As days at school got worse and she was fighting to keep her grades up and never heard from him for a long time but kept having visions of him and this girl Shelly and that he never fought to keep it with her but she knew by his feelings and his heart that it still belonged to her. She decided that she was not going to sit here and suffer and be in pain and so she let him go which was the hardest thing she had to do and so she lived her life as if she had never met him. But with as the visions kept coming and her heart wanted him and held on to him as well as the memories and dreams she knew that one day if it was right that they would be together but until then she was going on with her life.

The End was coming. . ...

After a good 5 months or so and with Timmy at the back of her head but the feelings still there and the pain of when he left. She went on with her life even with the visions of him and how he was doing good and with Shelly and loving her at a distance as well as Shelly and even though it was hard to see she knew that she was going to have to stop hoping that it would all change and go on and love again even though she didn't want to. So, after a few months of pain and getting over it all she woke up in a good mood for once and as she was walking down the street the next morning whistling and lost in her own thoughts, thinking about the assignments that were due that day from her teachers. She had worked on them ahead of time and so she knew that Mrs. Trisha Brown (English), Mr. James Shaggs (math), Mrs. Julia Barnes (Science), and last was Mr. Sam Green (P.E.) was going to call on her because they knew that she would have the answer to it all. She was very smart and had all A's in her classes, but that didn't keep her from living life and hoping that she would find someone to be more friends with. That day she was hoping to see a boy named Daniel Stanley and he was around her age and they knew each other since they were kids, but she knew that he would never be interested in her because she was not popular like he was but she still liked him and wished that she could get the strength to talk to him but she couldn't. what she didn't know was that someone else was in love with her and never told her but she kept getting notes in her locker from a secret admirer and even though she was taken by this, she was also scared because she didn't know this person or anything. As she arrived to school she was happy and curious to see what the day would bring, she walked through the doors of the high school ready and set for the day. She saw her girls outside on the terrace talking and joking with each other, she walked over toward them but saw out of the corner of her eyes that Daniel was watching her. She smiled and kept walking and when she got to her friends they were all happy to see her and they sat around and talked and joked around. Michelle started to look around so that she would not be so obvious but her eyes would always scan the crowd and land on Daniel and she would find that he was still looking at her. She couldn't help herself this time and so she smiled a very shy but sexy smile and then lightly waved toward him. He would smile back and wave back and then he would look at someone else and then gaze back at her but this time trying to make sure that she didn't see him. But she knew that he was starring at her, and she liked it but she knew that she would never belong to him or his world. She was the more dark and lonely type and it was what she liked, besides her friends anyway. Plus, with all of the pain that she went through a few couple of months ago she knew that it would never be the same and that even though she liked this boy she didn't want to be with him as much as Timmy but she only hoped as much that one day she would find someone that would make her happy and help her forget the pain that she went through to have her heart back on track and to love again, The bell rang interrupting her thoughts and so she went on to English and answered all of her teachers' questions when she would call on her and so it was a long day. Math was even more stressful, they had a quiz and then a test in a couple of days and so it never ended. Science was not as bad they were studying for a test but that one she was sure she would pass. P.E. was fun but also tiring and so she went through each class waiting for the bell to ring so that they could go home. Finally after all her other classes were done and the bell rand she ran to her locker only to find another letter and this time she looked around and after searching the crowd she saw a boy that was her age leaning against his locker looking down at something and when he caught her eye he quickly closed the book and shut his locker and took off down the hall and out the door. She knew this kid he was a nice kid but not her type at all, she felt good but at the same time she didn't want to hurt this kid but she wanted him to stop and so she wrote him a note saying that she was not interested and that he deserved better and asked him to leave her alone. She walked over to his locker and stuck it in through the slots in the locker and then walked away heading to her new model Toyota Camry. When she walked to her car, she saw the boy come out of the school with the letter in hand and saw his expression and how sad it was. She felt bad but she knew that it was the right thing to do, so she got into her car and drove home. As she was pulling out of the school parking lot an old mustang raced past her and cut her off. She was so mad but yet the boy behind the wheel waved and mouthed "Sorry". She let it go and kept driving to her house, when she got there she realized that the boy that had cut her off was the same boy that she had helped when Timmy was here and it brought back memories but she let it go and tried to forget it and when she arrived at her house she felt better and so she walked inside and sat at the table that was in the kitchen and started her homework and studied everything that was needed and then after a couple of hours she started cooking dinner knowing that her parents wouldn't be home for another week she made enough to last a couple of nights. She decided to cook chicken and rice and some mixed vegetables, after it was done and she took it out of the oven shutting everything off she made a plate then went into the living room where the TV was and sat down and watched her favorite shows. She got up about 30 minutes or less and put the food away and then went back to her shows. But as time went by she didn't realize what time it was until she looked at the clock and it said 10:00pm and so she took her dishes to the sink and washed them and then went up to her bedroom and changed into her Pajama's and then brushed her teeth and then crawled into bed wondering and hoping she would dream of the man for her. To her surprise when she closed her eyes, she saw black and clouds and then after a couple of seconds she saw a boy that was tall but adorable and he had blue eyes and short brown hair. But to her amazement in this vision he was kissing her and making her happy. She smiled at this but then she realized that the boy in her dream was the one that cut her off today and at this thought she felt discouraged but at the same time she knew that if it was fate then it will happen. She slowly drifted back to reality and then she opened her eyes to see that she was still at home and then closed her eyes again and slowly drifted off to sleep. When she woke up the next morning refreshed and waiting for the day to start, she was happy and singing to herself as well. She took a shower and decided to do her makeup different a little sexy and then she put on a red shirt and jeans and did her hair nice and then after she had her shoes on and everything she needed she decided to walk to school. She was feeling alive and happier than ever, school was only a couple of blocks so it was no big deal and so she walked down the street. She listened to her music and singed happily, and after she reached the park and watched the kids playing and the parents trying to get their kids in order she had to laugh, but she kept walking and as she passed the fence before reaching her school, she didn't see the Ford Truck that was a double cab and it was parked by a tree with a man inside and while Michelle was walking and singing with her IPod in her ears, that her father gave her last year for her birthday. The truck came out from around a tree and a street and pulled up to her and the man got out of the truck and came up behind her and caught her off guard, then he grabbed her and threw her into the back seat of the truck and sped off without a word and her screams were silenced in her mind but in the distance there was a tall,skinny,blue eyed boy named Charley Barrks that was standing against the tree a few feet where she was taken and as he stood there like a curious individual and not sure if he should get involved but within a few minutes past, he took off running in the direction of the truck and while he kept running he quickly turned into his true form and kept running until he caught up with them. He stopped at this old building that was torn and abandoned and saw the man carry the girl that was now out cold and brought her inside and tied her to a chair. The man also blind folded her so that she could not see his face, the beautiful Husky dog knew what was going on, and crept into the building without getting caught luckily and then he softly hid behind some boxes that were stacked against the walls and laid down so that he could keep an eye on the girl. But he also had every intention of watching the man as well, but he knew that he was not going to be able to intervene knowing that her life was going to be in danger and he hated that more than ever. He also knew from the day that he saw her that she was going to be his friend and maybe more and that he would do anything for her no matter what the cost. So, it pained him inside to watch this evil man torment her. His eyes never left the girl but now he saw that the man was asking her questions and when she refused to give an response he would sap her or beat her, as Charley thought good girl to himself and also be strong don't give in but then he regretted it because he saw the man slap her across the face so hard that she didn't turn her face forward for awhile and he growled very lightly under his breath not wanting for the man to hear. After a couple of days of watching the man abuse her by hitting her and punching her with every chance he got as well as making her tell her parents to pay a ransom. The beautiful Husky dog was getting tired of seeing this man hurt this wonderful creature as he saw it and so he was planning on acting on the next minute he could, he was in luck though within a few minutes of planning a way to save her, the man was pulling her to the truck and then threw her in the back while she was still blind folded and as he followed behind he saw that the man was not driving into town which was odd because he could hear the man's thoughts and he knew that the man was wanting to meet someone there to get rid of the girl but instead he stopped outside of town and found an opening to the sewer system and decided to throw her into the sewers like she was trash and after reading his plan he found out that the man was named Greg Brimmer. The beautiful Husky dog followed into the sewers after the man and watched him laying the girl in a corner and then the Husky dog sat in the shadows while the man left and locked the passageway with something hard and bolted the door as well somehow. The husky dog watched her suffer and cry as she tried to get out but he also remembered that the man Gregg was in his early 30's and supposedly to be very dangerous and full of hate and quilt.

A New Beginning, A new Love. . . . .

The Husky dog knew that he was not going to leave her alone in here but at the same time he felt like she was untrusting of everyone because of this man so he had to be careful but he knew that she was harmless and that soon she will be his friend he hoped anyway. When Gregg had picked up Michelle almost two weeks ago from school and told her that her parents were working late and paid him to watch her until they got off work. Her father Chris and her Mother Brenda owned businesses and companies all over the world. They were very powerful and rich. Her father and mother started their business at the age of 21 and married shortly after. Their business has grown since then and now with their business, they are able to control banks and other businesses. Greg Brimmer was an ex-employee of theirs and was known to be a trusted and easy going man and also a part of their family. They trusted their daughter and house to this man that has been there for them for many years. But as he kidnapped their daughter while they are working in another state to help their business, Things started to change. Greg decided that he is tired of being the one to do their work and slave over them. He decides to steal not only their daughter but their money. After he emptied their bank account and took their daughter to a dark alley way and tortured her until she was no longer awake and or breathing, that he was aware of. He then threw her into a sewer not far from his apartment and walked slowly to his door. His took out his keys and slowly turned the key into the door knob. Feeling nothing but satisfaction and fearless. He turned on his television and watched the news as we prepared a short and quick spaghetti dinner. After he was done he fixed his plate and then sat down on his couch and ate his dinner with the news filling the room. After seeing everything that was happening into the world and finishing his dinner he slowly began to fall asleep. Within 10 minutes he was finally asleep and preparing for the busy day ahead of him not caring of the trust that he had gained with the family and what he did for them or what they did for him and not even the girl.

In the mean time, Michelle slowly started to regain her strength as well as her memory and was slowly coming back to reality. When she opened her eyes and removed the blind fold all she saw dark and felt water and a strange texture under her nails and on her fingers. She then realized that she was not home and not anywhere that she was used too. She finally adjusted her sight to where she knew that she was in a sewer but she didn't know how she got here. She slowly got up and felt that her body was sore and bruised and bleeding from all the times he slapped her and hit her because she wouldn't talk and there were so many things that ran through her head but she knew that she had to be strong and so as she slowly got up and tried to walk along the wall of the sewer to find a place for her to get out. She searched everywhere and found so many ways out but she was not strong enough to push the latch on the doors above to the world outside. After searching for so long she grew very tired and weak and sat down on a ledge inside the sewer hoping that someone will know she is here and or come and fined her. After a couple of hours later she fell asleep against the wall and started to dream about her parents and wondering if they are looking for her. The next morning her tummy made a noise of hunger and she was thirsty, she slowly gets up and tries one of the doors. She turns and turns it as well as screaming for help. Unfortunately, it does not move an inch. She starts to get scared and worried if she will ever get out of here. A sound came from behind her and it startled her. She slowly turned to find a Husky dog starring at her. He looked to be at least a year old, she then slowly came down from the stairs that led to the door and slowly walked toward the dog. He softly made a noise deep in his throat to warn her not to go any closer. But she did not listen; she walked over and gently laid her hand on the dog's head. He snapped at her with his sharp and flaring teeth. Strike once and then a second time until the third his top teeth locked onto her arm and drew blood. She pulled back but then went to touch him again. Finally, the dog lay down and rolled over on his stomach begging for the soft touch and rub from Michelle. Michelle was scared and not sure if this dog would attack her unexpectedly again but at the same time she was glad to have someone or at least a companion to talk to. As she was in deep thought she softly heard the dog whine next to her. She looked down and gently put her hand on the animals head stroking him to reassure him that it is okay. He wagged his tail hesitating at first and then started to rapidly hit his tail against the cold concrete of the sewer making it echo all down the tunnel. Michelle slowly lay down next to the dog trying to get some rest before she started again on the doors, while she was lying there she thought to herself that she should name the pooch because she wanted to help him and keep him. She finally came up with a good name and leaned into his ear and said, "I'll call you Midnight". Midnight thumped his tail in happiness and let out a soft bark agreeing with her. She drifted off to sleep using him as warmth and slowly regained her strength for trying again to get free from this closed in and dirty place. When she awoke which felt like forever but it was only an hour later she saw that Midnight was pulling on her sleeve trying to get her to move with him. She slowly got up and walked with him and he stayed by her side. They walked down the sewers like a team on a mission as they also fought rats and dirty water and trash everywhere. Michelle was nervous and not sure where Midnight was taking her but at the same time she was excited and very curious. Midnight stopped in the middle of the sewers in a pathway that was closed off. Her heart started to sink knowing that it was a dead end. But all of a sudden she heard a noise above the ceiling of the sewer. She was filled with excitement and ran to the nearest door to the opening of the world above. She turned the door the best she could and banged hard and yelled, "help!!!!" A Construction worker that was working on the street with his team heard the noise and was not sure if he was hearing things or not but when he realized that he was not hearing things. He called one of his men over with the right equipment and told him to pull open the door to the sewers. As this man named Jason Mcbright and his coworker pulled open the door and when it was fully taken off he found a small girl dressed in a light blue dress with white shoes covered in dirt and dirty water from the sewers coming up towards the stairs with a dog behind her barking. She grabbed the man's hand and as soon as she was on the street she leaned down and helped Midnight up from the sewers as well. Jason quickly made sure she was okay by wrapping a blanket around her and midnight and then called 911. The cops were there within 5 minutes and were taking statements from everyone including Michelle. After everything was said and done she was rushed to the hospital with her Midnight at her side in the ambulance truck. They arrived to the hospital 10 minutes later and at first they fought her for Midnight going into the hospital but she stood her ground and told them that, that dog saved her life. They finally allowed it and as she was set up in her room and bed with the dog crawled up in the corner by her bed they both rested and was relaxed. The next day she woke up with her mom and dad by her bed. She was thrilled to see them as they were her, they had so many questions and concerns and when Michelle told her parents what happened her father immediately told the cop outside her bedroom door, the information that was from his daughter. Mr. Tj was a nice cop and he came into the room and asked Michelle to explain everything that she remembered. He wrote down everything she said and then after she was finished he turned to the father and said," this man that she talks about is a very evil and dangerous man; we will find him and catch him." He also said," I am going to have a couple of my men search your house and make sure it is safe and have them stand guard and protect you until we find this man." The family was grateful and as everyone was slowly starting to leave, Michelle looked at her parents and said," Mom, dad, can I keep Midnight?" Her parents hesitated at first but then realized that this dog saved their daughter and was mistreated before, so he looked like it. But what they didn't know was that he was healthy and stronger than normal and not what they thought. So, they looked at their daughter with confidence and happiness and both shaking their heads in agreement saying yes to her question. She jumped with joy and Midnight barked with happiness.

The hospital had reluctantly given him a bath so he was clean and looked better than he did before with his fur in knots and ruffled and smelled of sewer and trash. Now he was clean cut and silky and soft with his fur straight and brushed like it was suppose to be. Midnight jumped happily to the bed laying at the foot of her hospital bed protecting her and guarding her for any disturbance. Her mother and father sat on the sofa in the room letting her sleep waiting the next day for a new beginning. As the sun rose into the heavens and shined into her hospital bed she gazed out the window wondering what would happen now. Her emotions were confused and torn not sure if she would ever be able to trust anyone ever again, or to believe anyone ever again. As the room became lit from the sun she could see Midnight lying next to her parents on the floor of the sofa bed, her parents were lying next to each other peacefully. She quietly laid back down starring at the ceiling. It seemed like forever that her mind was wondering and searching for answers and contemplating her next move of how she was going to get through life dealing with this disaster and also how she was going to get her dog to be her's forever. She knew that after this dog saved her life her parents would let her keep it but at the same time she wanted to make sure she had a plan just in case. Her plan was to tell her parents she would do anything they wanted to be able to keep her rescue dog. As she was thinking she heard a soft "woof" and when she sat up and looked at Midnight it seems that Midnight's head was up and was watching her as her mind was pondering. Midnight tilted his head to the side as he watched her and when she just sat there and gazing back with love and care in her eyes, he gave a soft howl and it made her parents jump and wake up. They gazed at Midnight and then at Michelle and realized that she was awake. They got out of the sofa bed slowly and then asked, "Are you okay honey?" Michelle replied back, "Yes mom and dad" they sighed with relief and then stroked Midnight's head. His tail wagged and then he got up and walking over to Michelle and laid his head on her hand and nudged it with his nose. She stroked his head and gave him a little kiss on the nose and he backed away wagging his tail as he walked over to the window sniffing the air and then laid down below the window not that far from her bed. Her parents watched him and realized the commitment and the companionship that Michelle and Midnight had. Her mother and father then said, "Michelle You may keep Midnight on a couple conditions, one you take care of him and no one else, and two we need to get him some help since he was locked down there for a long time and we want to make sure he will be okay and won't die on us." Michelle smiled and replied, "Thanks mom and dad, and you won't have to worry no one will take care of Midnight but me." But what Michelle didn't know is that not only would she be taking care of Midnight but Midnight would be taking care of her as well. She also didn't know that she would be taking care of Midnight's secret as well. After a couple of days in the hospital she was ready to go home, and after four she was released to go home and rest. The next day she was taking Midnight to the vet and then her and Midnight was going to go shopping for dog supplies and then maybe the park on the way home. But for right now she was going to go in the back yard with food and water for Midnight and lay by the pool. She took a dish and put some food in it that was from a friend of hers that had a dog that she babysat sometimes and kept it in the house and then took another dish and put water in it. She got into her bathing suit and grabbed a towel and went out to the pool that was an in ground pool. She laid out her towel on one of the nice backyard chairs and then laid down basking in the sun. Midnight went over to the dishes and quickly ate the food that she put in the bowl and then went over to the water and drank the dish dry. He then walked over behind a bush and did his business. After shaking it all off, he then strongly and powerfully walked over to her chair and laid down watching the birds and trees moving. After a couple of hours basking in the sun she got up from the chair wanting some lunch. She went into the kitchen and made her a sandwich, Midnight was not far from behind her. For some reason she had this funny feeling that she was either being watched or someone was close to the house that shouldn't be there but she knew that Midnight would alarm her if there was someone close. She slowly ate her sandwich and her chips with a class of Ice Tea and gazed outside of the glass windows that surrounded the kitchen to the living room, and around the house. She could see her backyard from beginning to end and her pool was right in the middle taking a good portion of her backyards space. Her parents had it built not just for her but when they had gatherings and parties for their friends and clients; it was a nice warm and comforting place.

Trying to get on with Life. . ...

Her parents went to work every day even though they didn't want her to be home alone, she reassured them that if she had any problems she would go next door to her best friend's house or call them or the cops. But her parents were unknown of her new life that she was leading and taking over the city by destroying everyone that caused others harm as well as those that had hurt her. They were okay but still unsure with the idea; she was enjoying the peace and quiet time of the house and being with her Midnight. After she finished her lunch her mind was wondering if she should lay down for a bit or take a walk. Midnight thumping his tail on the floor by her feet gave a soft "woof" that made her think he knew what she was thinking. She grabbed her plate and put it into the sink and along with her cup and walked to the front door, As she called for Midnight and grabbed the door knob to turn it open, She got this strange feeling that she should stay inside the house. But knowing her and the fact that she was stubborn she didn't listen to this feeling and grabbed it and then opened the door. As she walked outside into the fresh air that smelled so nice, she saw a car that was an old model of a mustang and it was parked behind a tree a few feet from her house. She couldn't see who was behind the wheel but she knew that she would have to be careful because since she lived in a decent neighborhood she knew that whoever it was didn't live here. She slowly started walking towards her best friend's house and was watching this car out of the corner of her eye's and as Midnight was walking right next to her closer than he had ever done before she knew that something wasn't right. As she walked up to her best friend's house and knocked on the door. Midnight took off running toward the mustang, her best friend Carla opened the door with a smile and said, "Hey girl what's up?" Michelle said, "Nothing much thought maybe you would want to walk with me and Midnight to the park for awhile?" She turned around to find that Midnight was not there and so she called for him and then told Carla "He's my dog and he was right here but he must be chasing a squirrel or something?" Carla laughed and replied, "We will find him, just let me grab my coat". Within a few minutes Carla was walking out of the house with her coat and they were calling Midnight and trying to find him before they headed toward the park that was only a couple of blocks down the road. After a couple of minutes of calling him he showed up right by Michelle panting heavily and wagging his tail and then they continued walking and laughing and then started talking about boys and like always Michelle's mind was on that car. Carla realized that Michelle was not paying attention and then asked, "Michelle is something wrong?" Michelle dazed and thinking snapped back to reality and said, "I'm not sure, I'm a little worried about that car that was in front of your house and mine." Carla thinking for a minute and then said, "Oh yeah the mustang, it has been sitting there since you got back from the hospital a couple days ago." Michelle stopped and said," WHAT!!??" Carla then said, "Yeah you didn't know that?" Michelle then moved her head back in forth saying, "No" and her mind was spinning in all kinds of directions. She then looked at Carla and said, "Do you know who it is?" Carla said, "He looks like a teenager maybe 15 and very cute." Michelle knew that Carla was boy crazy but for some reason she didn't have a good feeling about this. Michelle was not boy crazy and never really wanted to be in love, she knew one thing though when she gets home she and this boy were going to have a talk. They got to the park and Midnight was running around playing fetch with kids and enjoying life as Michelle and Carla sat at a nearby bench. They watched him as he played with the kids like a puppy, and then talked about everything that happened in the past week or so. She had been out of school for a long time and it seemed like forever, Carla was telling her of her new boyfriend crush and that he didn't know she even existed which was normal for Carla because even though she was pretty with her stylish clothes and blue eyes and red curls, she always seemed to either fall for the wrong boy or always got hurt but she kept on like nothing happened. This time the boy's name was Jeff and he was in our grade and new to the school, she said, "He has blue eyes like me and brown short hair and wears jeans and plain shirts every day." Michelle just laughed and said, "Sounds like your type of guy." They both laughed and then Carla said, "Michelle can I ask you something?" Michelle looked at Carla and said, "Yeah sure what's up?" Carla paused for a minute and then asked, "What type of boy are you looking for?" Michelle smiled, knowing that Carla meant well and then said, "Well looks don't really matter to me, it's how he treats me, and I want someone that would take me anywhere just to spend time with me and someone that would treat me like their queen." Carla listened and then said, "Wow, maybe I should raise my standards." They both laughed and then both sat back on the bench watching Midnight trying to chase a squirrel which made them laugh even harder. After a couple of hours they got up called Midnight to come on which he did quickly and then strolled down the sidewalk to go home. For some reason she had this feeling to turn around, and when she did she saw the mustang just sitting there watching her every move. As they walked to the end of the street and the mustang did not move, she finally turned around and walked straight to the mustang. Carla watched and walked in her direction to keep up.

When Michelle got to the mustang she was shocked to find a cute boyish looking 15 year old with blue eyes and short brown hair wearing torn jeans and a blue shirt. He looked back at her and she did him, she then said," why are you following me?" He smiled, and then as she looked at him she said, "You are the boy that I saved that night and you cut me off a couple times aren't you" He smiled and then said, "Yeah, I guess I am, I never got to thank you that night, so Thank you" She smiled because this boy was tough but also cute and someone that she could see herself with but she didn't want to think of that now since she was still trying to get on with her life and not love anyone that she had too. But as she looked into the boy's eyes she wanted to know him inside and out and it was started to get at her but as she stood there and watched him she smiled and waited for him to say something. He smiled at her and then Said, "Your father asked my father to ask me if I would keep an eye on you and make sure that you are okay and that no harm would come to you after what had happened to you before." She stepped back and then leaned back forward onto the car and said, "So, My father has told you then, what happened to me?" He looked down and then said, "Well, he told us that you were kidnapped by someone that was close to you all and so you don't trust anyone no more, but that is about it" She relaxed and then said, "Well, that true but he also beat me and abused me and threw me into the sewers to die and if it wasn't for my dog Midnight I would not have made it out a live" the boy softly said under his breath "I know I was there" She heard him say something and then she said, "What?" the boy looked up and said, "I'm sorry Michelle, I wish I could take him out of the picture for you, but maybe soon" She looked at him because she didn't know that he would say anything like that and then she said, "Well, I will have to ask my father if you are telling the truth." She was trying to change the subject and then the boy said, "Why would I lie to you?" Michelle said, "I don't know? But I don't know you so why should I believe you?" The boy said, "Good point" He stuck out his hand and said, "My name is Charley Barrks, I'm 15 and go to high school not that far from your school." Then he pulled out his phone and dialed a number and handed it to me. I took it uneasily and said, "Hello" I heard my father's voice and said, "Hey dad I just wanted to make sure that you sent Charley here to pick me up and to keep an eye on me". My father without a doubt in his voice said, "Ah, yes his father is a good friend of ours and we thought that he would be good to be your friend too while your mom and I leave on trips." I paused and then said, "Oh okay" then I said, "dad, am I allowed to hang out with him whenever". I could hear the smile cross his face and then he said, "Yes, honey we trust him and you so have fun and we will see you when you get home." I smiled and then said, "Okay dad have a good day and see you later I love you". He said, "I love you too honey" and hung up.

I saw the twinkle in his soft blue eyes while I handed the phone back to him that made me want to wrap my arms around him and never let him go but my heart and battled each other as I slowly walked to his car and got into the front seat of his car. I turned around to see him still beaming out of excitement. This made me scared but I stayed where I was because I had a feeling that this Charley was harmless. He moved into the driver seat and sped his wheels trying to show off and then stopped and hit the gas pedal and we took off down the road at a fast speed but I didn't care because I felt free for the first time and I was enjoying every minute of it. I opened the window and let my face feel the breeze and my hair flew against the wind and came back and would hit my face as we drove down the small streets of the unknown. I looked up at the sun of the afternoon and then gazed at Charley and saw that he had a smile at the corner of his mouth trying to escape. I wasn't going to give him any gratification so I smiled back and was wrapped around the smell of the earth and the wind again getting lost into my own thoughts and before I knew it my eyes slowly closed and I was a sleep for the first time since I had been home. It felt like a short couple of minutes but when he slowly touched my arm I felt his warm touch and was awake before I knew what hit me. We were stopped at my house and I noticed that the lights were off so my parents were not home. I grimaced as I started to get out of the car and walked to my front door not realizing that he was right behind me carrying my stuff. I turned on a light and was whistling for midnight knowing that he would have to go out and that he was hungry. I was terrified that he didn't come and felt this bad feeling overwhelm like a blanket suffocating me not letting me breathe and in that moment I turned toward Charley he was putting my stuff on the bright red couch that my mother had to have. He looked up quickly looking very concerned from my face. I just stood there not being able to move and then out of the blue I started running up the stairs and to each room yelling his name not knowing where he was. Charley watching me unsure of what to do, finally, he grabbed my arm in mid air and slowly wrapped his hands on either side of my face but I tried to pull away because this felt strange but at the same time it felt right and then he said," Michelle, what is wrong?" I took a deep breath and then with looking into his eyes I was surprisingly calm and then I replied, "My dog midnight is not here." Charley leaned back not releasing his hands from my face and then said, "Oh, Your parents brought him to my house so that I could take care of him while you were in school." I stopped and then said, "how when you go to school too?" He smiled, then he said, "I only go on certain days" I said, "OH" I felt uneasy as his hands remained around my face and I felt a feeling that was unspoken of, like there was a connection there that neither one of us both knew of. He suddenly felt my body tense up and smiled and then leaned back and said, "You have the prettiest eyes that I have ever seen." My cheeks turned bright red and felt this tingling feeling run down my spine. He laughed out loud and released me allowing me to be unstable and before I could catch my balance he already had me by the arm helping me. He looked at me concerned and I smiled and said," I'm okay you just made my heart jump a beat or two." He smiled but didn't let go of me. We stood there for a few minutes and then finally he said," well, since your parents won't be back for a long time I would like to show you something if you want to come with me "I hesitated and then I said, "I don't know if I should but as long as you really want me to hang with you". He looked at me questioning my comment. I have never had anyone that wanted to hang out with me or even look at me with passion in their eyes. Then he said, "Why wouldn't I want to hang out with you?" I smiled, then said, " well, I'm not the best looking girl that has blue eyes that shine like most do and my hair is dark brown not red or blonde like some girls do, I'm skinny but not great looking like most girls so I don't know to me I am ugly and just blah to all of the guys here" I was laughing inside until I saw his expression and for the first time I felt like everything that I just said meant more to him then I thought. He walked over to me and said very firmly, " now, Michelle you listen to me okay I have met many girls that are crazy, wild, and just way out of my league and I have had my heart broken more times than I could count on my fingers so don't think for one second that you are ugly and you are worth everything in this world" He took a breath and then said more calmly, " Michelle, what I am trying to say is that every time I look into your eyes I get lost and feel happy and that has never happened to me before and for once in my life I have found someone that makes me happy and that is enough for me the question is it for you." I couldn't move or breath as the words ran through my veins and that minute or two I felt like I was going to fall and just start crying because one no one has ever said anything like to me and made me feel beautiful but at the same time I was scared because I never felt anything for anyone before.

The New Love. . . . . .

I stared at him for a few minutes and then said, "Charley no one has ever said anything so beautiful to me and I thank you" He smiled and said, "Your welcome honey" we were silent for a couple of minutes and then he said, "come on I want to show you something that is second beautiful from you" I blushed bright red and then said, "okay". We walked out of my house and I locked the door with him right behind me watching every move I made as well as the neighbors staring at us in interesting questions in their heads but I didn't care because for the first time I was free from my pain and the world that had hurt me in the past and being with him had changed it all and I had a friend that I knew would always be there for me as I would him. I got into his car and he got into the driver seat with confidence and we drove off leaving everything behind and not the care in the world. The whole time I was wondering where he was taking me because I had no idea and then after enjoying the breeze and the presence of him the time seemed to be going by fast because it felt like 10 minutes and then he started to pull over on this dirt road and as we drove through the forest I could smell the trees and hear the animals at a distance that made me feel free from everything and then he parked his car in a dirt path that was leading the woods into this open space that separated the woods from this whole other world and as we got out and walked through the path I could see this path of rocks as well as grass and then a river and when I looked to the left I saw this small waterfall that was so beautiful that it took my breath away and then to the right of it was another land that was unknown to me for sure. He took my hand and we walked to the left of the river and walked up on rocks until we came across this smooth rock with a grassy patch that we could sit there comfortably on it. We sat there in silence taking everything in and then he looked at me and smiled and I smiled back. Then he said, "I come here every day to think and relax what you think?" I smiled again and said, "It is beautiful and I hope you will share it with me" He looked down at me and said, "this will be our spot forever if that is what you would like sweetheart." I smiled and nodded in agreement, We sat there in silence and then I slowly started to lay back against the grassy patch and when I did I fell with a thud with my arm behind my head and Charley turned and looked at me and did the same thing I did. He laid down right next to me rest his arm behind his head and as we gazed up at the sky, lost into our thoughts but then it went by so quick that I didn't realize that he was resting on his elbow looking down at me and when I realized this I could see his eyes gazing into mine and then he said, "would you get mad if I kissed you?" I smiled up at him and said," No, I wouldn't." I didn't know what was happening to me but I knew that every minute with him Timmy no longer was there and the feeling of him was gone and the love but I knew that I would have to tell Charley and so before Charley reached down to kiss me I sat up and stared at the trees and this got his attention and he looked at me and said, "What is wrong?" I turned to him and said, "Charley, I need to tell you something before you kiss me or before we get close, I was in a relationship a while back and fell in love with this boy named Timmy and his stepfather killed his mother and then his father came and took him away from me and went to Atlanta, Georgia and he promised me that after graduation that we would get married but after he left he stopped calling me and fell in love with someone else." I sighed and then said, " I became angry and bitter and hurt, I never thought that I could love again and I tried to get on with my life but I still have feelings for him and dreams of him and visions and so I just want you to know this so that you can decide if you really want to be with me or not" He looked at me and then said, "Well, I know that he hurt you, but I promise you that I would never do that to you and if you really want to be with him then me then I can understand that but it sounds like to me that he has moved on and so I think that you deserve better than him." Michelle didn't know what to say to that and then she said, "You know you are right, I tried for so long to keep the love strong and the hope and in the end I only hurt myself worse than if I had just let him go to begin with, so I am going to move on with my life and forget him the best that I can anyway." He smiled his big grin and then leaned down to me and pressed his lips to mine and as we kissed my whole world felt like butterflies flying uncontrollably everywhere and then when he released me I felt like the world had crashed. I laughed at this thought and he looked at me. I smiled and said, " I'm sorry you did nothing wrong I was just laughing because it felt like butterflies were everywhere while our lips were together and then they weren't it felt like the world crashed. He smiled and said, "Like this" and he kissed me again and I laughed again once we released lips again. And then I said, "yes like that" He laughed too and then said, "you know Michelle I felt the same thing when I was kissing you and I find it to be a good sign" I was still looking at him and then I said, "same here Charley and thank you for helping me with this problem and being there for me". He smiled at this thought and then lay back down and then without question he pulled me to him and I had my head rested on his shoulder with my hand on his chest and we both gazed up in the sky again.

Before I knew it I had fallen asleep in his arms which I never thought that I would be able to do that with another guy ever again but as I slept with him holding me I felt peaceful and full of hope and love and soon I could feel that he was lightly shaking me trying to wake me up. But I was so lost in sleep that I was dreaming or at least it felt like I was and the last thing I knew he was kissing me on the head and picking me up in his arms and carrying me to the car and without thinking I wrapped my arms around his neck and buried my face into his cheek and neck still asleep. I could feel him pull me from him and then I realized that we had gotten to the car and then he kissed me again and put me into the seat and buckled me in safely and then I vaguely saw him walk around the car to get into the driver side putting on his seat belt on as well and starting the car and driving out of the path his car was in and then heading to the dirt road that led to the road and then I noticed he had laid his hand on my leg and It felt so nice and comfortable that I didn't move or moved it, and I drifted deeper into sleep then I have been able to do since that night that evil man took me away from everything that I knew and loved and since the night that Timmy left me. When I woke up I was laying on something soft and warm and had something even warmer on top of me, I saw the sun shining into the window of a room that was not mine, I started to panic but then realized that I was in his bedroom and then relaxed back into his pillows as my eyes started to wonder the walls and the dresser and the pictures of his family everywhere I assumed they were anyway. I sighed a little and then I heard a soft snore that came from the bottom of the bed and on the floor, which it sounded like to me anyway. I was curious and so I crawled with the comforter still wrapped around me to the end of the bed and leaned my head over and saw that Charley was sleeping on the floor with a pillow and a blanket. I had to smile and when I did I saw his expression and it was the most beautiful I have ever seen so peaceful and happy and so I crawled out of his bed and crawled over to where he was sleeping, trying not to wake him I laid next to him wrapping his free arm around me when out of the blue he jerked protectively but still sleeping and he smacked me in the face. It felt so hard that I jumped back and screamed In pain and his eyes flew open unaware of what happened and when he turned to me I saw someone else and I started to crawl backwards toward the door and he never took his eyes off me and within a second I saw Charley and he moved his head back in forth as if to clear it and then he looked at me and said in a sweet voice, "Michelle, what happened?" I couldn't speak I was too scared and then out of the blue I screamed at him " Charley all I did was try and lay next to you to cuddle with you and your arm around me and YOU HIT ME, YOU HIT ME CHARLEY" I didn't even take the time to see the horror in his face I grabbed my stuff and threw open his door and barreled down the steps out of the front door still wearing my tank top and sleepy pants but I didn't care I walked down the street to my house which was a long way at least 4 or 5 blocks from his but I held my hand to my face in disbelief that the one person that I trusted and knew in my heart that I would love hit me. I would not have been mad if it was done with less force as if I had scared him but this hit was more of a fierce hit like in a fight or when animals get at each other's throats. I was walking so fast in my own world that I didn't realize that Charley was running after me yelling my name over and over again. Finally for some reason I stopped walking and just leaned against a tree and started crying. He stopped in front of me and tried to take my face in his hands but I threw his hands off of me and he would put them back, finally after fighting with him he made me look into his eyes and said, " Michelle, I am so sorry I was dreaming of the man that hurt you and I grew angry and in my dream I hit him and in real life it was you, I didn't mean to hurt you my dear I promise with all of my heart I would never do anything to hurt you" then he said, "Please Michelle forgive me I will do anything to make up for this or anything that I have done to hurt you." I just sat there looking at the sun not sure what to do or say, and within this time that I was shocked and thinking of what to do I realized that I never told him what that man did to me. This made me scared and I saw him in the corner of my eye and he was getting on one knee begging me for his forgiveness. I looked at him through hurtful eyes and then finally got the words to speak, "Charley, I never told you about what that man did to me or anything and I don't care what dream you were having or what might be happening I saw a different person behind your eyes that scared me more then you slapping me and that I don't know what to do or think of ...."but then something came over me and I stopped and then said realizing that he was waiting on me and then I said, " Charley You ever do that again or hurt me at all I don't think I could live with it nor be able to sit here like I am without falling apart so please promise me that I am safe with you and that you will never hurt me again" Then I said, "Charley I gave my heart to you when I didn't think that it could be possible and my heart can't take it again and I just hope that we can make it work and get passed this" He stood up and walked closer to me then he has ever been and took his hands and wrapped them around my face as I gazed into his eyes and knew that what he was about to say was from the heart and that he was not lying to me. He kissed me passionately on the lips and then when he released me he said, "My darling Michelle, one your father told my father and me what happened to you and two I promise that I will never hurt you again, I also promise that you are safe with me and that I would die for you whether it be keeping you a live or my life over yours or for any reason" he paused and then said, " Michelle, I know this is early but I think that I am falling in love with you and I know this sounds crazy but it is true and I wish that you could just feel and see what I am feeling" I hesitated and then felt my heart jump and I knew that I loved him too. I spoke clearly and strongly at this point and said, "Charley, I can't do this right now I am hurting inside to the point where I don't know what to do, but I would like to take what we have slow if that is okay" he looked at me hurt but then with understanding eyes and then said, "Do you want to go back to my house?" I hesitated and then said, "Sure". We walked to his house holding hands and then when we reached his door about 15 minutes later I took a shower and got dressed and when I came out of the bathroom he was waiting for me outside of the door. I looked at him in wonder and then he smiled and said, "you are so beautiful sweetheart, I can't believe that I have the best girl ever" I knew from his remark that it could have meant girlfriend or best friend but I didn't care I just walked toward him like this morning never happened and he walked toward me like this morning was gone forever and then we were locked at the lips again and we never wanted to let go then he took my hand as we started to separate from each other and then he walked me down the stairs and when we got to the kitchen and near the table and it was dressed with a beautiful pink table cloth with two white candles in the center of the table with two plates and a knife and spoon and two forks in the right places next to the plates as well as glasses but then I saw that he arranged the plates one across the other so that we could look at each other. I gasped with a soft noise and leaned against him as if to say how wonderful and he kissed me on the lips and then brought me too my seat and when I sat down he poured me a coke in the glass as well as one for him and then pulled our lunch out of the oven and rested it on the table under a pot holder and then went back to turn the oven off. He came back and served the delicious potatoes and vegetables with a wonderful pot roast. He sat back down and we ate in silence for a couple of minutes and then he reached over and took my hand and held it while we looked at each other and ate our lunch. I then looked at him again and said, "Charley I was wondering what are we?" He looked at me and said, "what do you mean love?" I said, "I mean are we friends or are we dating to be together forever?" He smiled and then said, "oh that, well, I want to be yours forever and be only yours so I guess what I am saying is that I want to be your boyfriend and one day your husband" I blushed so red that I looked like a cherry and then I said, "well, I only want you and I want to be your girlfriend and yours forever" He smiled and then frowned and looked down at his lunch and said, "but not my wife?" I realized that he did not know how I felt about that but I wasn't going to tell him now. I looked at him and said, "maybe one day but I don't want to talk about it now because I still feel like I can never get passed me belonging to someone that wanted me and then didn't and so I have to be sure and all that is important is that we are together" He nodded and then kissed my hand and then put it back down.

The Truth comes out......

I felt weird because I wanted to tell him but it wasn't the time since we moved kind of fast but we knew that it would work out or we wouldn't be together and also because we kind of skipped breakfast but that was okay because this would make up for it big time and this moment with him made me feel like a queen more then I could ever ask for. I didn't want this day to end but I knew that I was going to have to go back home again, he saw my expression and I saw his and then we smiled and finished our lunch. When we got done cleaning our dishes we walked outside too the fresh air and took a ride into the city and just chilled with each other before I had to go back home to my empty house, which I was not looking forward too because I knew that I would go crazy. We walked in the park for a couple of hours while everyone looked at us while we held hands, but we didn't care. As they were walking with Charley she had this funny feeling to go home and so she pulled Charley in the direction of her house and when she got there she opened the door to find a man and a boy sitting at the counter eating their food. She knew that her life was getting more and more complicated and soon she knew that it would get worse and that even she had found that person that she could love for the rest of her life but she wanted to make sure that what she was doing was right and lasted as long as it needed it to be. She doesn't want to lie to anyone but she knew that the way she dresses and the way she walks with stride and confidence as well as no fear what so ever she knew that she was going to kill and save who she could until the time came for her to stop or live her life. She kept getting these visions of her fighting the world as she stood here and for some reason she didn't know why but before she could speak to the intruders she remembered the dream she had that night of all the bad in her town and found that there was more in the world, but she was determined to make sure that it ended. She realized that Charley was beside her and that the two people were strangers, and knew that her parents would have told her if someone was coming over. But when she turned around she saw that the front door was not open and nothing seemed out of place. She got ready and not sure how to approach them but she turned the corner and then said, "Excuse me what are you doing in my house?" She saw the man and the boy jump from the voice and the man said, "I'm so sorry we were told that we could stay here and we have been traveling for days now." Michelle said, "Who told you?" The man could see Michelle by the wall and then he smiled and said, "Well, a man that we crossed paths with and unless I have the wrong house I could have sworn he said here." Charley tensed beside her but he said nothing and Michelle's body was tensing and then went from unsure to anger and soon she was in full war mode and while she tried to control herself she walked out into the hall and with her expression and body stiff and ready to fight. The man saw this and said, "I'm so sorry miss I think we have the wrong house." She couldn't speak because she was afraid that she would scream out a curse and so she nodded yes and then when they started to leave she relaxed and when they were gone her emotions went back to normal and she was no longer in war mode. Charley kept by her and let her fight this until she needed him but then She walked over to the window after the door closed and what she saw was so amazing that she knew that whoever they were, they were like her. The man and the kid was making a cat dance with nothing but their minds and then the kid being mean ran it up a tree. She laughed and then thought she would try something before they got to the car they were driving in. She closed her eyes and thought to herself, why are you here? And what do you want from me? The man turned around when she opened her eyes to see and then he replied, "Only to help you, your parents were dear friends to me and my wife and son and I told them that we would help you with anything, they just didn't know what we were or what you were but we did. She thought "oh, well you guys can stay as long as you want, just don't do anything in front of others. The man nodded and they headed back to the house, she was unsure of this still but she knew that she could use these two for something, whether it was answers or to help her save the city from crime and hurting people. She knew that it would be okay because Charley was beside her and would be with her no matter what she hoped. He felt this emotion and kissed her hard and said, "Always". She smiled and then took his hand and they all went into the living room to talk and figure things out.

After the quests left after a couple of days and answering her questions of her life and future and helping her best they could. Charley and Michelle walked around enjoying the outside and then it hit me where was my dog. I looked at Charley and he looked at me confused at my expression, then I said, "Charley where is my Midnight" He blushed and said, "He's fine I promise" I looked at him and said," Charley we should have brought him with us?" he looked down at me for a minute and I could tell that he didn't know what to say to that. Then he said," Yeah we should of but I really wanted to spend time with you a lone and not have to worry about him chasing other people or growling at someone that got too close to you, you know" I stopped in place and looked at him because what he had just said was strange it was like he could read or feel the same thing that midnight did, it was like charley was him. But that couldn't be because midnight is a dog and Charley is a human and that just can't happen. I ignored my thoughts and we kept walking until we reached the best place to go for dinner and that was a country place that was not far from the park that everyone went there. We sat outside because it was a nice day and we ate our dinner in silence which was odd to me but I didn't push it. Then he paid the bill and he took my hand and we walked down the street looking for something to do. After starring at the stars on a park bench for the longest time and being happy. Then I felt him pull me down the road and into this store that were for girls and told me to pick out anything that I wanted. I didn't know what to say or do because he had given me so much already that I felt like I was taken advantage of him. But he insisted and that he liked buying me things so I told him that we would pick it out together and this made him happy. He pulled me to something that I figured he had wanted to buy me for a couple of days now but was not sure if I would wear it or approve of it. I looked at it through the glass and it was beautiful it was heart necklace that was gold and the heart was red like filled with passion. I saw the price and gasped because it was $800.00 and I couldn't believe he really wanted to get it for me. I looked at him and he was gleaming and happy I said, "Charley that is a lot of money" he smiled at me and then he said, "Michelle, I know but you are worth it and I want you to have it" I didn't know what to say. I smiled at him and then said, "do what you want I know I can't change your mind but just remember that I will pay you back somehow or another" He smiled, then he said, "Oh Michelle, if you only knew how much you have paid me back already, just by being with me and being my friend, and hopefully more it is the best gift I could have asked for. " I smiled and he paid the cashier with cash and then he took the necklace out of the box and put it around my neck and fastened the clasp. I looked down at it and was sucked into its beauty, I looked back at him and smiled and then I said, "Thank you Charley I love it" He smiled, then he kissed me and said," Your welcome honey I'm glad, now you have my heart forever" I blushed and then kissed him again and this time I couldn't help myself but then I said, "Charley you have my heart forever too, I then rested my hand from my heart to his on his chest and he breathed in and then out and then kissed me again and said, "thank you Michelle that is all I want and need" We walked out of the store and walked toward my house. It was closer than I thought to his but it was still farther when you are walking. We walked hand in hand until we reached my front door and when I went to open the door I got this strange feeling wash over me, Charley was watching me and I knew that my face was horrifying looking but I gasped and sat on the porch with a thud and then Charley was right down with me and he was afraid by my face that he was lost of words for a second then he said, "Michelle, are you okay?, What is wrong?" I took a deep breath and then said, "Charley I don't know but I have this bad feeling not to step foot in my house. He realized what I meant I don't know how but he did and this time he stood up strong and squared his shoulders and went to the door with the same face that I saw in his bedroom, full of hate and anger towards someone that hurt the love of his life. He turned the knob with determination and stepped inside shutting it behind him.

Scared...

I was so scared and not sure what to do but I didn't move I just sat there scared and then after 10 minutes or so I realized that I could lose my best friend and the man that has ever been good to me so I stood up ready to face my fear, I was just about to turn the knob to the front door when it flew open and the man named Gregg went flying across the yard and hit the lawn with the biggest sound I have heard. I was thrown back out from the door flying open and landed on the porch and hit my head against the railing but stood up and was shocked that I found Charley standing in the doorway with the same angry face and when he spoke I was even more scared. His voice was deep and angry with no remorse and no feeling at all. He looked right at Gregg and said, "If I ever catch you near her family or her again I will kill you, you hear me you no good.........uugghhh your not worth a breath of anything, get out of here before I decide to dispose of you now." Then he stood there arched like he was ready to race after him and strike him again, Gregg stood up so fast that I didn't see him running down the road to his car on the other side of the street sign. I didn't move for a couple of minutes until Charley came over to me and wrapped his arms around me to where my head rested on his shoulders. When I looked up I saw that his face had changed and was calm and my Charley. I relaxed and then he bent down and kissed me and then he said, "Baby, your safe now he will never hurt you, not as long as I am around" I started to cry and then I said, "I know Charley I don't know what I would do if you weren't here". He pulled me closer to him and said, "Baby, are you alright, I saw you hit your head?" I smiled and said, "Yeah" He said, "Well, you're safe now and you know that all you would have to do is call my name and I would hear you and be right by your side in a heartbeat. I ignored the truth behind this response but I kept holding him. After a few minutes he said, "Baby would you like to go back to my house for awhile I will call your dad and explain everything it will be okay." I moved my head back in forth as if to say yes and then we walked off my front porch after locking the door behind me and I felt him behind me and for the first time I wanted him to touch me again, not understanding why since I had never been this close to a guy or had one so determined to make me happy or protect me. We walked to his car and he held the door open for me and shut it when I was safely in and had my seat belt on. He walked around the car to the driver side when I realized that he was walking funny but with a stride that I never noticed before after all the time we spent together but then it hit me I think that he was trying to hide it from me knowing that I would be worried or judge him even though he knows that I am not that type of person. I gazed at him and when he got in I couldn't stop looking at him. He looked at me after a couple of minutes and said, "Is something wrong I mean I know I am not that good looking?" I blushed and said, "Actually, you are the best looking guy I have ever seen, I can't believe that you would take the time with a girl like me or me actually because I'm not that pretty." I paused and then said," I was actually wondering why you were walking funny?" He smiled, then said, "well, first off you are beautiful and I find that every second I am with you I never want to leave, and as far as the walking funny I have a hip problem because when I was just a young one I got hit by a car and was in the hospital for a long time and so it will be there for awhile." I stopped and then took my hand and laid it slowly to his face and caressed his face to feel this soft skin, I saw him relax and lean into my hand and realized that he was enjoying it as much as I was. I went to pull my hand away but he took it with his free hand for the second and lay in on his leg while he drove. I hesitated because I felt funny but he kept his eyes on the road and kept driving and I never moved my hand and for some reason I felt this hot burning sensation that made me want him more than anything in this world. As we reached his house it was white and a two story with a beautiful fenced in back yard and the front had trees that hovered the house like wings on each side near the street then when you walk up the walk way you entered a big front porch that led to the door that was white and wooden. Inside was white walls that were filled with pictures of the family and it was decorated as if someone had professionally made it for a queen. The couches were red velvet with a lovely dark wooden table in the middle the couch's been made to be facing each other and to your right at the end was a fireplace. Then right in front of the door was the stare case that led to the two bedrooms and a bathroom but then when you looked to your left there was a room that had a kitchen table all of oak and a chandelier that hung from the ceiling made of crystals and through the room you entered the kitchen that had a door way and in the kitchen there was a refrigerator bigger than the counter and then in the middle was a bar counter of wood and also in the middle was a stove with cabinets that held everything in place. To your right there was the sink and the dishwasher and the normal things on the counter like the coffee pot and tools for cooking. Past the bar and refrigerator was a little space that you could sit and lounge and was another four chaired table of oak. Then it opened up into the main room with the fireplace that was so wonderful the house made me feel like I was meant to be here forever. Charley came up behind me out of nowhere and I had been so amazed with the house I left him at the doorway not realizing that I went wondering around. I looked up at him and blushed and said, "I am so sorry I just had to see the rest I never saw it the first time because I was a sleep and this house is beautiful." He smiled and said, "It is okay we get that a lot but my grandpa built this house and I am hoping one day it will be mine." We walked up to his room and he put on some music as I sat on his bed. He sat next to me and I could feel his body tense as I moved to make myself comfortable. I looked at him and said, "What's wrong, did I do something I shouldn't have?" His face went silent and for the first time I could see pain and confusion in his eyes. He looked at me and said, "Michelle, I have never had a girl in my room nor have I been in any relationship with one, so this is hard for me." Then he said, "My life is complicated so it is hard to give my heart to anyone and it gets to the point of frustration because I feel like it is going to end before I will be ever to live it right and find the one that will understand me and understand my life as well as accept it." He paused and then looked away from me leaving me short of words as well as feeling helpless. He stared at the floor as he said, " Michelle, I don't want you to be scared and feel like I am crazy but I have to say this so please don't hate me or run away" then he said, " For the first time in my life I have found the one that I want to make happy and spend every waking moment with, you have made my heart flutter, my eyes to never want to look away, every protective emotion and muscle in my body become more realistic and come into play, I have never felt this way for anyone and I don't want to let you go." He stopped for a second and within that minute I realized that he was really meaning that he wanted to be with me and that he would do anything to win my heart. I gasped at this thought and didn't realize that I did this out loud until I saw him jump and look at me faster than I have ever seen someone look me. But as I looked into his eyes I saw that he was serious and also worried and for this I knew what I had to say. I took a deep breath and then said, "Charley I have had a hard life and year so far not sure of what my life will bring, not sure if I will ever be able to trust another person again or love another person again because the man that hurt me was a good friend of my parent's and I knew him since I was born and then all of a sudden he takes me away and hurts me to the point of darkness." Then I said, "But for the first time since what had happened to me when I saw you waiting for me today at school I knew that my world was going to change for good and I knew that you were the one that was going to pull me out of this and protect me from everything and for this I also know that I will trust you and love you every day of my life and you will be the only one." Then I said, "But I need you to promise me something." He never stopped looking at me and watching me and then he said, "I promise to love you, to protect you, to make you happy, to be there for you, to trust you no matter what, to give you space when you need it, I will do anything for you." I smiled at his words as they filled me with a warm feeling that made the darkness I had been feeling slowly disappear. Then I said, " I promise the same, but I also need you to promise that we will take our time with the relationship because I want it to be true and I don't want us to get hurt if one day it changes and so promise me that we will take our time and enjoy every second of it." He leaned forward and took my face into his hands and said passionately, "Michelle, I promise with all of my heart, I also promise to never leave you, to never hurt you in any way for I can't be here without you by my side." I smiled as his hands were caressing my face and then he leaned further to kiss me but something told me to draw back but for some reason I wanted it so bad so I leaned in toward him and when our lips touched it sent a shock wave through our bodies like we were finally together after so many years. When our lips separated we leaned back and smiled at each other again, he let his hands fall and then got up to walk to his dresser I felt a lone for once but soon he was back and as he took my hand I could feel the warmth from his body as he opened my hand and dropped something heavy in it. I looked down to see a silver ring in the middle of my palm and for a few minutes I just looked at it. He slowly took my chin and raised my face to meet his and said, "I want you to wear this if you will, but nothing will change about our promise, I just want you to have something of mine." I smiled and happily put it on my finger and shockingly the only finger it fit on was my wedding finger. We both laughed and then kissed again. He wrapped his arms around me and I leaned into his shoulder and he kissed my hair and as we sat here for a good time he finally said, "What would you like to do now my dear Michelle?" I smiled, "Charley I was wondering if we could go for a walk or go somewhere beautiful and talk". Charley relaxed more against me now and I knew he had a smile across his face when he said, "I know just the place" he took my hand and led me outside the door of his room down the stairs past the kitchen and through the back door toward the woods and we ran for the longest time hitting every tree and living thing in the forest it felt like. Then finally I got to take a breath and when I looked up from pressing my hands on my knees there was a field that was at least a few miles long and across the field there was a tree that had a old tree house that was his I assumed. We ran to it and climbed the steps that were nailed to the tree and sat on the bed that was in there and there were walls but for some reason there was no wall facing the field so we could sit there on the wooden floor gazing out at the field at a distance and see everything a live and not moving around. I didn't care as long as we were there together. We sat there in silence and then he wrapped his arms around me and then he said, "This is my hide out and where I come for peace and quiet from the pain and complications of my life".

A Different World. . ..

My heart and mind wanted to know more about what he meant. I looked up at him and said, "Charley what do you mean complications?" his body tensed up and looked at me and then said, "I was afraid you would ask?" I got scared and kind of moved away from him but he pulled me back and said, " Michelle there is something about my life that no one knows not even my parents and I have had this gift since I was a small kid but it didn't develop until I was about 8 and I never knew how to control it or what it was from until I was ten, this gift is something that was brought on me from nothing I know of, I know just how to live with it and live my life the best that I can, I am afraid that if I tell you will not understand and never talk to me again or want to be near me either and if I have to keep it a secret to keep you with me I will." This time I took my hands into his face to make him look at me and then I said, "Charley I am with you 100 percent no matter what it is and what I feel for you will never change or die, and trust and no lies or secrets go with it." He looked at me with concern but understanding eyes as he took a deep breath and said, "Michelle, remember when you were in the sewer and you found a friend that saved you from that nasty place because that man put you in there?" I tensed up as he brought this up and then something hit me, he was talking about midnight. I shook my head in agreement and then he said, "Michelle, I am midnight" I stared at him in shock and when I saw his eyes meet mine I could see midnight looking at me and then I took my hand pressed it against my chest in shock and I saw him look away and then he said, "I told you, I knew I should never have told you." I let my hand fall and then I took his chin and had him face me and then I said, "no, I am glad you did I knew there was something special about that dog but I couldn't put my finger on it, Charley all I care about is that I found you and that you want to be with me everything else is a part of who you are and I just want to know everything about you because that is what is important to me" I paused and then I said. "Charley it will take me some time to get used to it but having you with me and loving me is everything that I could ask for." He looked back at me and said, "I do love you and I want you to be mine and to be with you forever that will never change." I smiled at him and said, "That's all I need, everything else will work into it and it is a part of you and so it will be for a long time and I am willing to accept it and understand it as you do and that is all that matters." He smiled and then leaned forward while my hands were still holding his face and he kissed me firmer this time and then took me into his arms and relaxed as we sat there in silence and after our lips separated I could tell by his body he was saying thank you and so with mine I tried to tell him that his secret was safe with me and he got the message because he hugged me tighter and nodded his head in agreement and then he kissed me again as we sat there holding each other.

As we sat there I realized that there was a question in my mind that was bursting to be said. Charley sensing this looked at me with curiosity and said, "Baby, you can ask me anything that you want?" I felt more relaxed and so I asked, "Charley baby, I was wondering what makes you transform into midnight? And does it hurt? What do you feel?" these came out of nowhere and I felt like I was stepping my boundaries but he looked at me with love and then said, "okay first off, I transform when each emotion that takes over whether it be hate, angry, or fear and most of the time it's when I feel like someone is in danger I protect the streets at night which is mainly when I turn. It used to hurt but now it is natural as if the animal inside of me is being unleashed, and then lastly I feel everything." He paused then said, "Baby, I feel love, hate, sad, lonely, bitterness, it's like I feel what people are thinking or saying but there are no words and even though I can't read the minds I know that what I am feeling is real because it is like my own feelings" When he stopped I was looking at him and was full of wanting to know more. He chuckled at my face and then he said, "I wish I could show you but I think you would be scared sweetheart" I didn't know what to say to this so I just cuddled closer to him and kissed him on the lips and then buried my head into his chest. He gently stroked my hair and ran his fingers through it and it felt good until he stopped and tensed up. I sat up but he pulled me back down and out of the corner of my eye I could see these two guys walking in the woods and looking forward in our direction. I got scared and grabbed him tighter to where he could not breath but he softly whispered in my ear "I love you and I will let nothing happen to you" To my surprise these two guys were right under us and they were walking funny, I realized that they were drunk. They finally turned around when they kept walking and within seconds they were right in front of us. I was starting to feel better when one of them yelled to the other and said, "Yo Gus it looks like this kid is getting lucky tonight with this chick" The kid named Gus Strong turned around and said, "Yo kid is there any room for us up there" The two boys busted up laughing like it was a joke. I heard a deep growl come from Charley's throat and it was scary enough. The two boys were walking towards us now and at the same time they said, "Oh, you think you can take us huh?" I snorted at this comment and for some reason I said, "Stupid boys he would tear you apart and if I was you I would run as fast as you can and disappear like that" after that I snapped my fingers together and it made a snapping sound and with my surprise the boy named Gus was thrown a few feet away from the tree and landed on the ground with a loud sound that made us all jump. The other boy named Ralph Lawrence busted out laughing and still came closer to us. Charley looked at me with shock but held me tighter and then said, "whatever happens run" I looked at him and said, " I'm not leaving without you" He said very firmly " yes, you are I don't want you hurt and to see me change" I stood up strongly and said, "Baby, I'm not going anywhere I love you and we fight together" The two boys laughed even harder at this and tried to pull me down by my shoe but I kicked him in the face and broke his nose. The Ralph tried to grab me and got me when I tried to fly off the tree house but while I was trying to fly, I ended up going backwards and hitting the wooden floor of the tree house and hitting my head on the floor. I could see Charley getting angrier then before and while he tried to help me up, I bounced back and swung my feet to get me up and when I landed back on my feet I swung forward and jumped off of the tree house and landed with a thud on the ground and took running toward them. They didn't move for a minute but after they saw my body ready and my face instead of running away they ran to me. Bad Idea, but they kept coming and I knew that this was it I was ready to kill them with every feeling and emotion that came over me and after a couple seconds my brain was racing and processing everything and soon I was moving my arms and my hands and fingers faster than ever and it was like they were commanding orders to destroy these no good pests. Gus went to swing at me and as soon as his punch went for my face, it was like slow motion giving me the advantage of fighting back and he missed but as soon as it hit air. I took my fist and swung it to his and when it hit his teeth and mouth the power and force was harder and heavier than ever. He went down faster than anything and never got back up. But as I was waiting for Ralph I could feel Gus getting back up slower and so I didn't move fast enough and he took my legs right from under me and I landed on the ground with a great force and before I could get back up he was on top of me trying to pin me down and trying to take my clothes off of me but I knew that this boy was not going to get that chance. I grabbed him with such force that it made him scream and flung him forward and he went flying in the air and hitting a tree harder then I hit the ground and then I got up laughing in a very sadistic rhythm and then I turned sensing Ralph behind me but as soon as I saw him coming for me I saw Charley in midnights form running behind him and leaping through the air and before Ralph got to me which I was ready Charley landed on him and tore his throat out and within seconds he was dead. I couldn't believe it but at the same time I didn't know what to feel because the feeling that was inside was confusing and harsh. Charley looked up at me with shock and confusion as well. I looked back at him as a

2

different person just like he was looking at me. My first reaction was to run and that was what I did, I ran into the forest not sure where I was headed or what I was going to do because whatever this was was not me. I ran so fast and not looking back that I forgot that I left Charley but I needed time to think. I kept running and my mind was able to come together and cope but I knew that my parents did not know about this and I wasn't sure about other family members so what else could do. Finally, I got this feeling and as I was running I could see a vision of my grandfather and Uncle that were next to my parents and in my vision they were telling me that they would come to me, all I had to do is ask. I felt strange but I answered the vision and told them to help me, they agreed and said to expect them at the end of the week. They told me that they would train me the best that they could but first they would have to teach me about the gifts and how to control them before anything else and so I knew that it will be awhile before I would be able to really be controlled and safe from others but I nodded to them and then ran even harder and soon I was back to the place where I left Charley. I saw him standing there on all fours in his true form and just gazing in the direction where I had started running and then when he saw me his body relaxed and then he came running to me and whining because he thought that I left him for good. When I was in front of him I took my hand to his head and kissed him more deeply than before and said, "I would never leave you no matter what" I saw his mouth turn up and it looked like a smile and because of this I smiled as well. Then I said, " Charley, I'm so sorry I needed time to get my head back on track and to find answers to what just happened to me" I paused and then saw him full of questions. I smiled up at him and then said, "Go ahead ask me?" He gazed at me and then he said still in dog form which was amazing, "Michelle what was that? Who are you? What are you? I never saw anything like that in my life." I smiled and said, "The only thing that I can tell you is that I am not normal and that my grandfather and Uncle will be here to answer my questions at the end of the week so then we will know." He looked confused but then nodded, He walked toward me and at first my instincts told me to walk away and never come back but my heart stopped me and so I walked toward him and he shifted back to himself and lifted me up so gracefully and light and it felt wonderful and carried me and as I drew closer to him I felt peace and love. I didn't think it was possible for me to wrap my body around his because I thought he was bigger than I had thought but I could and I felt safe and unscarred and he was mine and that was all that mattered, I looked behind me and realized that we were running away from the fort and all I saw was pieces of the two boys lying on the ground. I looked at my clothes and saw that one got my top ripped almost off and my pants were torn as well. Charley, made a growling noise in his throat as he ran toward his house and as he ran like he could feel what I was thinking. I stroked his cheek and kissed his neck and then his throat and he stopped as he knew that I was trying to make him feel better but he was still running. We finally got to his house and he sat me down on the back porch and then went sat down next to me then I said, "Charley you don't have to worry about me getting hurt because I don't get hurt or at least I don't feel it away" He grabbed me and hugged me tight and then kept kissing me. When I could breathe he looked down at me and then with my chin level with him so that we were staring at each other he said, "Michelle, I don't know what gift you have but I will never stop protecting you and loving you, and so it is my job to make sure that you are not hurt and safe from those idiots in the world." I giggled and kissed him harder and then said, "Oh yeah" He nodded at me and then said, "Well, Charley it is my duty to save you and keep you safe from those idiots as well, plus the enemies that may come after me and so I guess we are team then" He hesitated but then knowing that I was not going to let him do it alone and he wasn't going to let me. He opened his mouth to speak and object but then smiled and said, "Yes my love we are" I smiled and then kissed him hard and he returned the kiss. It was kind of strange having him holding me with no clothes on but at the same time I couldn't stop touching him but when I realized what I was doing I pushed him back and looked at his face and it was Charley and then I said, "What's wrong Baby?" Charley stopped and then He sighed and then said, "Michelle, When that kid started to pull you toward him and I couldn't keep you in my hands I thought I lost you and then seeing you fighting him like you were used to this made me even more angry that when I changed to help you and to save my one true love I turned into the beast that you called me, not a dog a beast and it scared me" I didn't know what to say to this but wrap my arms around and him and hold him. Then he said, "I killed Ralph Michelle, I have never killed anyone before" I could tell that he was scared and so I said, "Baby, I'm sorry that you had to do that I wish you didn't have to but they were going to kill me and try to kill you so you did it in self defense" he tried to smile and then said, "Thank You sweetheart" He hugged me closer and then kissed me like he hadn't seen me in forever. Then he looked right at me and said, "I don't know what I would have done if anything happened to you my darling Michelle" I smiled and said, "I don't know what I would do without you either" we both smiled at this and then kissed again. He picked me up with his arm around my waist and then carried me to his bedroom. His parents were not home which I felt like I should meet them but I knew that I will soon.

A New Experience. . ...

As we walked in the house and he took my hand and walked me up the stairs to his bedroom. He sat me on his bed and then He kneeled in front of me and started to gently take off my shirt I wasn't sure what to do but his soft skin felt so good that I didn't stop him. But after he took off my shirt and left my bra that was still intact I could see what he was looking for. I had cuts and bruises from the fight all cross my chest and arms. He looked at me with pain in his eyes and I took his face into my hands and said, "Baby, I'm fine and I am even better that you are here with me and touching me" He leaned forward and kissed me and then walked out of the room to the bathroom. When he came back I had laid back on his bed to relax. He came back with a kit to heal me back up, then he sat on the bed next to me and said, " Michelle, I have never wanted anyone like I want you but I respect you and love you and I will not do anything further unless you were my wife" I sat up shocked at this and said, " so, what you are telling me is you will kiss me and hold my hands and hug me but nothing more unless I am your wife" he agreed with me and I couldn't believe that I was going to have to break my own rules just to be happy. I am not the type to get married and be stuck with one person even if I love them, I am not the type to wait that long to get what I want but for the first time in my life I wanted more with Charley and I would and will do anything for him and to make it work. He looked at me and then said, "Are you sure this is what you really want?" I looked at him in disbelief and said, "Charley I have never been so sure in my entire life" He smiled and said, "Okay baby, I promise I will make it worth your wait" I felt lost and confused because I always promised myself that I would never give in for anyone no matter how bad I wanted to and as I sit here I was giving in to him and unsure why. I mean I knew in my heart that he was the one for me and that I wanted to be with him for as long as I could but the other feeling was how I know that it will get that far. My mind was spinning with thoughts and so much confusion that I didn't realize that I was staring at the wall deep in thought. I saw from the corner of my eyes that he was staring at me with concern and came back to reality. I smiled and he kept staring at me and then finally he put his head down and looked at the floor and took a deep breath and then said, " Michelle, I feel your sadness and uncertainty and it makes me unhappy, so, if you want to be closer and intimate then I will not reject you because I love you and you are the only one that I want to be with and touch I just need you to know that this is going to be hard for me because you are my queen in my eyes and I know that once you are mine and our hearts are one that the day we become one together will be a better day" He stopped and waited and when I didn't say anything he continued and said, "If this is what you want then I will do it for you, but I am scared for many reasons and one is that I don't know how far this gift of mine will go and I don't know what will happen either" I looked at him and then said, "Charley I don't know what I am either but I know that I have the power to control it and to keep you safe as well but what I don't get is that you would rather wait till like our honeymoon?" He stopped realizing that I made sense and then said, "I would wait until I knew more information about this gift or curse before taking a chance on hurting you" I stood up and walked to his window that opened it up and walked out onto a patio and leaned against the railing looking at the moon and got lost into my thoughts. He came up behind me and wrapped his arms around me and I tensed up not sure if I wanted him to touch me while I was deep in thought. I realized that he felt this and he backed away from me and leaned against the railing next to me. I kept staring at the moon and he kept looking at me. After a couple of minutes I turned and looked at him and finally said, "Charley,

I am not the type to get married to anyone I don't like the idea of being controlled and not free but since I have met you I have realized that you are all I want, but for me to sit here and wait and going against what I believe in and desire and trying to protect myself for the longest time." He kept looking at me and then I said, "Why, this is so important to you besides of what might happen? Then he said, "I am afraid I will hurt you for one like I said and I am afraid that everything will change between us and I don't want that to happen? I leaned closer and put his forehead to mine and looked into his eyes and said, "Charley, I promise that the only thing that will change will be that we are closer than ever and as far as you hurting me we can take it slow but I know that with my gift whatever it is that you won't even leave a mark" He was hesitate about this but then he said, "Michelle, I will make you a deal, we will do this but if there is one hint of me hurting you or us changing for bad then we wait until later okay" I agreed and said, "okay" I smiled and took his hand and pulled him to the bed and he smiled when he saw my face and then said, "Now?" I said, "Tonight we kiss and cuddle and touch" he smiled and agreed. I sat down on the bed and waited on him as he started to crawl toward me and I couldn't help myself but giggle a little as I saw him moving to me with love and passion. When our faces met he smiled and kissed me and then slowly took off my shirt and threw it across the room, then I took off his and threw it and didn't care where it landed but saw out of the corner of my eye that it just hung there in the middle of the air until it slowly drifted to the floor, I watched it while his body was against mine and I was smiling but amazed at the same time and then he was even closer to me gazing down on me, I felt like the weight of everything was on me and I didn't realize how strong he was until at that moment. I could feel the heat coming from his skin and body and I could also feel his heart beat against mine as they were beating together in harmony. I sighed out of satisfaction and when we were so close he started to kiss me then my neck and down my chest to my bra. I didn't move but just started to kiss him back the same way and then ran my fingers all along his body. After a few minutes I could tell by his face that he wanted to go further and I looked at him giving him permission and that was all I had to do before it started to get wonderful, I hadn't planned this but I was glad that it was going to be more and it made me happier than ever to have all of him.

An Interesting but Passionate Feeling. . ..

I could tell that he was trying to hold his emotions together because I could see him go from Charley to Midnight in front of me and it was hard for him. His face would change into midnight that determined, powerful, and fearless creature and then his face would change into that worried, loving, protective Charley. He would relax and kiss me even harder and then turn back thinking he was in control and then in a split second he would change again trying to stop and protect me but I was not scared at all. He started to kiss me from my lips to my ear and then slowly move down to my neck and chest, every inch of me wanted him more and more ad then I found my body relax and asking for more. I saw him smile and then he slowly stroked my body while kissing me from my breast to my belly button. When he reached the part of me that wanted him even more he stopped, I looked down at him and then was about to say something but he continued and soon I could feel every inch of me out of control and besides the heat and warmth and love and passion I was feeling for him he came back up and then I knew that I was ready and that he should never stop at all. He could see this watching me but kept trying and soon I rested my hand on his shoulder and wrap my body around him as he slowly was deeper inside of me and when he realized this he tried to pull back but I pulled him closer and after he realized that I was stronger he relaxed and then his form changed into Charley and when we were done his body flexed and then rested against me out of pure tiredness. We fell asleep that way and it was great, when I woke up I was dazed and didn't know what happened. I looked down and saw that I was naked and he was lying next to me but I was not hurt because I was stronger than him. I looked over at him and made him look at me and then I said, "Baby, I'm fine you didn't hurt me, did I hurt you?" He smiled and said, "No baby you didn't, but next time please don't force me so far into you that kind of scared me" I smiled and then said, "Oh, sorry" I giggled and then kissed him as he kissed me back. He laid closer to me and wrapped his arms around me then he kissed me again and it was the best feeling ever. After a couple of minutes he said, "Baby what would you like to do today?" I smiled and said, "anything as long as it is with you and that I don't have to go home to a empty house" He smiled and then his face went ridged as if that day came back to him and then he said, "Baby, you don't have to go back to your house unless you really want too because your father told me that he wants you with me every day when they are gone and my parents are okay with it as well" I grabbed him tighter and then said, "good, I don't ever want to be separate from you" He smiled and then looking down at me and said, "Never". I smiled at this and then said, "Baby we need to go to the house so that I can pack some clothes" He frowned and then said, "I will go and bring your clothes back for you" I said, "okay but hurry back" He kissed me got dressed within seconds and jumped out of the window hitting the dirt with force and before I knew it he was half way through the woods running toward my house. I lay back down and against his pillow on his bed waiting for him to come back when I heard sounds that I thought were coming from the house or outside when I realized that they were inside my head. The next thing I knew I could see the guy that hurt me and he was planning his next attack against me and my family and in that moment I felt helpless but at the same time I was there and this vision was so strong that I couldn't come out of it. I didn't realize that Charley was back within 15 minutes but as soon as he saw my face he dropped my stuff on the floor and ran to me trying to shack me back to him. I shooked my head and he said, "Baby, what is it?" I didn't know what to say but then finally I said, "I had a vision and I could see him planning another attack against me and my family and it is worse than before and in the end someone will die but I don't know who" He grabbed me and said, "Baby, I will not let anything happen to you I promise." I shooked my head in understanding but he never let go of me. I buried my head into his chest and he ran his fingers through my hair and kissed me constantly. Sweat was coming off my forehead and body as he held on to me and then for some reason I felt him stiffen not realizing that I had went into another vision and this time it was worse than the first one. I was tied to a chair and he was hitting me over and over. He had ripped my clothes off and kept hitting me and torturing me and then as I watched I saw my parents tied down in chairs as well and they had to watch him doing this until he killed me. I screamed out loud when he had killed me and when I did this Charley jumped and then when I touched him it was like he saw what made me scream or felt it. He got up so quickly that I almost fell off the bed but he caught me and then sat me back down and then started pacing back and in forth. As Charley kept walking back and forth it made me uneasy. But I knew that he was trying to plan something and then my stomach turned as he looked at me and then I knew that whatever it was not good. He then said, "I will fight for you and die for you and so I will go see this man and dispose of him as I should." Fear ran over my body knowing that I might lose the man of my dreams and heart. I stood up and walked over to him and said, "I can't lose you; my world would never be the same, plus remember we said we are team now." He understood but I knew by his face that his mind was made up He said, " I know baby but please let me do this, I will get my friends together and we will take care of it and be back sooner than you think." Then I said, "When?" He saw me start to tear up and said, "Tonight, I will not have him take the one thing that matters away." I started to cry harder than ever and he came over to me and kissed me and then said, "I love you with all of my heart and you will never lose me, I will be back." After he kissed me the last time he was gone when I looked up. I had to take my mind off of it. I didn't know if he would be back or when, so I took my clothes out of the duffle he brought me and took a shower then got dressed and then went downstairs and had some cereal and when I was finished I sat down on the couch and watched TV while I waited. Then after a couple of minutes I got up and made sure that all of the doors were locked. It seemed like forever and then as I sat on the couch everything went dark and I could see the man in his apartment and he was sleeping waiting the new day of horror he was planning. Then in that second I saw Charley crouched against the wall in full form with two others next to him and they attacked him in his sleep and he didn't know what hit him but it was shocking, they tore him to shreds not even hesitating and once he was dead they left in silence but I saw that Charley was planning to leave me to find who he was. I felt horror and bitterness but at the same time I felt peace and hope wrap around me and then came back to reality. After 20 minutes of the vision and it going away I heard Charley come in through the window in his bedroom and came downstairs looking for me. When he saw me he smiled and said, "Your safe now baby no one will ever hurt you again." Besides the blood that was all over him. I looked at him and said, "Except you." He looked at me and then said, "what do you mean?, did you have another vision" I said, "yes I saw you and two others kill him but I also saw your thoughts and that you were going to leave me." Then I said, "Thanks but I can take care of myself and I don't need someone to defend me if they don't feel that I should be with them either" I was so mad and hurting that I didn't know what to do. He looked down at the floor and said, "It won't be long I just have to find out who I am so that I can control myself and so that we can be happy together." I grunted and then stood up and walked upstairs and grabbed my stuff leaving some behind but I didn't care and then walked downstairs and to his front door and he stood right in front of me and said, "baby, please don't leave me, I need you here." I looked right at him and said, "Apparently you don't need me if you were planning on leaving me behind." Then I said, "I love you, Goodbye Charley." I slammed the door in his face and walked down the long road that led to my future.

Betrayed. . ..

As I walked down the long road, forgetting about my grandfather and Uncle coming in a couple of days which I decided to pull out my phone and call them. My Grandfather picked up the phone and when I told him what had happened he said, "Michelle you shouldn't be a lone and even though you might be mad at him right now, you need to go back until we come down." She listened and then said "Grandpa, I know that you are worried about me but I can handle myself and I think that you should wait until I come back to come down." Before she listened and let him argue about it she hung up the phone and turned it off. She knew that she would come back but she needed time to think and get her head straight before she went back to Charley and the love she had for him. I headed East but not knowing where I was going to end up but kept walking and it felt like forever. The sun was setting and falling and then it got dark and then the next thing I knew it was morning. I kept walking east until I couldn't walk any more and then ended up resting for a whole day sleeping in the forest where I felt safe and then started walking the next day again and then to my surprise after a couple weeks I came across this big town that was nice and interesting and it was Atlanta, Georgia. I realized that I was where Timmy was and wondered if I could try and find him, and so I walked around the streets unsure of what I was getting myself into but didn't care at the same time. I walked into a store and asked the clerk if they knew a Timmy Oxford, the clerk looked at me and then he said, "Yes, who are you?" I smiled and said, "My name is Michelle" He looked at me and then said, "Wow, I have heard a lot about you and if you can wait a couple of minutes I will bring you to him" She nodded and then sat down outside and waited for this guy to get off work, she wasn't sure she should go with him but he seemed harmless and seemed like he knew Timmy. When he walked out about an hour later he led her to his ford Truck and then helped her buckle her seat belt and then got into the driver's seat and then drove for about 10 minutes and when he stopped she saw this little house that was white and looked very small but nice. They walked up to the door and he rang the bell. A man answered the door and she realized that it was his father, then when he saw her his smile got big and then said, "Come in Michelle, come in" He led her to the living room where Timmy and his girl friend were and a couple other guys as well. Timmy looked up from the TV and when he saw her he stopped and took his arm off the girl that was sitting next to him and he jumped up and ran to her. He stopped in front of her and said, "Michelle, what are you doing here?" She looked at him and said, "Well, Charley and I had a fight and I left to clear my head and walked for days almost a couple weeks and found myself here" He put his arm around her and then said, "You walked here, are you crazy?" She laughed and then said, "Oh, if you only knew that you don't have to worry about me, because I'm tougher then you think" She saw that the he remembered her visions and how she fought and saved people. He nodded and then said, "Let's go outside in the backyard" She followed him and saw that his girlfriend was watching him and did not like the idea, but she kept following him and when they reached the backyard, he grabbed her and tried to kiss her on the lips. She pulled away and said, "What are you doing Timmy?" He looked down and said, "I miss you and I'm sorry I couldn't call, I have been in a situation and not sure how to fix it" She looked at him and then said, "Like what?" He looked back toward the house and then said, "Well, the girl that I have been with is the daughter of a mob guy and she is always jealous of me and doesn't trust me and I can never get free from her and I want to be" Then he said, "I don't know what to do, because her father threatened to kill me and my family and the people that I love but I can't be with her anymore, I don't love her." She looked at him and then said, "Well, I don't know what I can do to help you, because you got yourself into this and I found a guy that helped me through my hard times and I love him" Timmy looked at her and said, "I love you Michelle and I haven't forgotten about our promise together, and I want it to come true" she sighed and then said, "Timmy, I can't I have already told Charley that I will be his forever" Timmy got mad and said, "You promised me first" She nodded and said, "I know Timmy, I know but that was a long time ago and we are different people now" She saw Timmy shake his head back in forth and she knew that she wasn't going to get anywhere arguing with him and so she turned to leave when he lightly grabbed her arm and turned her around to face him again and then he said, "Please Michelle, don't do this to me" She sighed again and said, "Timmy I will always love you that will never change but I can't do this right now, I have to go" Timmy sighed and then said, "Please don't go, stay for a little bit longer" She couldn't even though she really wanted to. She wanted to take him away with her and love him and make love to him but she knew that she couldn't do it no matter how bad and she knew that it would hurt Charley more then she would want and so she turned and walked away. When she reached the door she saw the girl standing by the door and watching them. When she opened the door she turned to girl that was trying to hide and she said, "Let me tell you something sweetheart, that boy is the best thing in the world and if you hurt him or if I find out that you send your fathers men after him I will come back and kill you and your family you hear me" the girl looked scared at first and then she looked evil and mean and she said, "Oh, really well we will just have to see about that, you have no idea how powerful I am or my family" Michelle laughed and then said, "Oh Yeah, well you don't anything about me honey and trust me I can make your whole family disappear in a matter of seconds." When she got to the door she felt that she should show her a little demonstration and to make sure that her message got across because she wasn't lying she would come back and kill her and her family. She turned around and faced the girl and with a couple of seconds in her mind she wanted the girl to feel pain and so she found the girl's thoughts all hateful and full of jealousy and soon the girl was on the floor screaming out of pain and holding her stomach and her body. Everyone ran to her to see what was happening and when they realized that Michelle was the one doing it they backed away and watched because that was the only thing that they could do. Timmy watched out of pleasure but at the same time fear, and then when Michelle released her the girl got up and turned to Michelle and said, "You are crazy, you could have killed me" Michelle laughed so hard that it scared everyone and then she said, "Well, if you do anything to hurt Timmy and his family, I will" She turned and walked out of the house feeling refreshed and better then before and even though she let her anger out on the girl she didn't care because she deserved it. She walked for a couple hours before she sat down on a bench and caught her breath when a tall dark haired boy sat down next to me and was staring at me. He finally said, "How are you? Never seen you hear before" I finally got the words to say and said, "My name is Michelle and I just walked from Morehead City, North Carolina and I have never been here before" He smiled and said, "well that is a long distance my name is Trevor Johnson and I have been here all of my life so if you want I can show you around and you can also stay with me and my brother and sister if you want" I nodded my head to say "yes" and then as he stood up I went with him and then we started to walk toward his house and I had to stop because my legs were hurting and so was my body. Trevor turned around and without asking he picked me up and carried me the rest of the way which I was glad because it was a longer walk then I thought. We reached his porch and it was a nice white house with a huge white porch with rails that went all around the front porch. He had one brother and one sister, there was Neptune, Alexia and they were all around the same age. Neptune was 18 and his sister was 17 and he told me that he was 17 so they were very close. They came outside to see who he was bringing to their house it seemed like, He put me down as we reached them and he spoke to them in another language that I did not understand at all. I never heard of it and so this made me feel funny but at the same time he made me want to smile all day long he was so handsome and I could stare at him all day long. He had green eyes and dark black hair that was long in the front but short in the back and his two brothers were the same except for their eyes which one was brown and the other was blue. His sister was beautiful and just amazingly attractive one had red curls that fell to her back with blue eyes .They didn't speak at first but then when he was finished explaining something he smiled and then they smiled and they were speaking English and telling me to come in the house. I hesitated but Trevor pushed me forward, I walked into the house and it was just simple with white walls and a couch and fireplace and windows everywhere, there were 6 bedrooms for each of them as well as one for me and there were three bathrooms but the house was nothing compared to Charley's. As this thought hit me my heart fell into my stomach and I stopped moving and then everything went black and I could see Charley talking to his parents and they were telling him the story of his gift and curse and I could tell by his face that he did not like the result but I could also feel his emotions and I could see that his heart was hurting because he let me walk out the door and he knew that he would have to fight for me but a feeling of love came over me because I could feel that he was prepared to fight and sacrifice his life for me. My heart fluttered and my stomach and mind were yelling at me for being so stupid but I was stubborn and ignored it. I then saw him packing his clothes and telling his parents that he had to find me and that I was all that mattered to him. His parents didn't fight him they just said to be careful and then I saw him leave with his things and head in a different direction then I took. The vision went dark and when I came back everyone was looking at me with confusion but at the same time I could tell that they knew what I had just had. Trevor stood me up and then His sister Alexia asked, "Did you just have a vision? " I hesitated because I did not know these people but I said, "Yes, my boyfriend and I had a fight and so I left and just kept walking until I got here and so I had a vision of him trying to find me" They looked at each other and then Alexia said, "well, if you want to be with him you may but we believe that since you are one of us that you should know a little bit about your gift and what you could do before you decide" I was shocked and confused and said, "what do you mean?" Alexia said, well,

I will show you and then if you have questions then I will answer them" I didn't know what to say or do but I found myself very curious and so I followed her and she took us to this trapped door and pushed the statue to the side and it revealed a stair case leading to a dark basement type place and as I am walking down the stairs with a torch to light the way I was thinking to myself what did I get myself into. As we reached the bottom I could see pictures of witches and wizards and potion and tubes lined in their racks on a table and believe it or not a caldron that was filled with some kind of potion that had smoke coming from it. I looked around the room to find that what she was trying to tell me was that I was a witch like them. I didn't know what to say but then I turned around to Alexia and said, "Are you all witches?" She laughed at this and then said, "Ages ago our families have tried to find the word for us that are not like the rest and it just so happens that we have inherited it from my parents and we have researched and found that our gifts are not common and so we have also found that we are witches but with a lot more than most have". I stood shocked and unsure what to think at the same time and then I said, "What makes you think that I am a witch" They all looked at me and said, "Our grandmother Lucinda gave you the same gift as her and our beloved mother before she died" out of curiosity I said, "what are you all talking about?" Trevor frowned and said " Maybe you should sit down for this" I felt my legs start to shake and so I sat down on the couch and Trevor began the story and said, "A long time ago a woman named Heather and her husband Harvey Bentz had a little girl and our grandmother visited her in the hospital before she delivered and told her that the little girl will have danger follow her but she will be strong and outlive us all, and so she passed away the next day , as she gave everything to you she knew that you would be strong and do the right thing when you got older and then later after you were born your mother died giving birth to you and well your father was killed by My brother Neptune" I looked at Neptune and the tiger inside wanted to rip his head off and I could see it as if it really happened. Trevor then said, "one more thing Michelle, your adopted parents don't know this story or about your real parents so eventually you would have found your way here"

Then he said, "If you would like I can take you to your old house tomorrow or anytime that you would like" I looked at him and then said, "I want to see it soon" He smiled and then said, "Okay, anything for you" Then I looked at them all and said very harshly "What makes you think that I will believe you and for that matter join you" Trevor looked at me understandingly and pulled something out of his pocket and it was a locket that inside held a picture of me and my mother and father. The anger burned inside of me and before I knew it I had gotten up from the couch and had Neptune pinned against the wall to where he could not move or fight back. My eyes were dark as my heart and then I said, "Why did you kill my father?" Neptune trying to find the words said, "I went back for you but someone called the cops and so I had to leave, my goal was to bring you back here and we were going to take care of you and teach you everything and be your family. Then he said proudly, " Our mother and grandmother could see the future as well as see what was happening now and change it and feel emotions and read their minds at the same time and she could also look at the moon and see the inside of it like taking her visions and putting it into the moons hands and making it the heart of the moon and change anything she wanted, she was very powerful but never got to see how powerful before she was because she was killed just like our father" I took this in and said, "well, as far as I am concerned you are all murders and you can go to hell" I threw Neptune across the room and he landed on the kitchen table crashing it to the floor and then I stopped dead in my tracks and then was staring at Alexia and she was serious and I looked at her with hate and pain and I closed my eyes and reached her mind and then started to cause her pain and she flinched and screamed out and I was about to kill her when Trevor put his hand on my shoulder and said, "I know you are mad at us Michelle but please let what we told you sink in" He let go of me and then I let go of Alexia and she ran to Neptune's side where he was on the floor. Then I asked, "How do I know which powers to use and how do I use them?" Alexia relaxed and then said, "We will help you and have you practice every day and soon you will be unstoppable and then we would love for you to join us and be a part of our family if you don't kill us first" I smiled and laughed and then said, "when do we start?" Alexia pushed a smile and then said, "Tomorrow morning at 8 am because we need to keep it all silent because it could cause problems is this town and so we don't tell people we are witches or even do magic in front of them" I nodded and then said, "Okay now what?" They all laughed at me and Trevor said, "What would you like to do?" I said, "Can we go for a walk so that I can see the town?" Trevor said, "Sure, I'll take you" As we headed toward the stairs and as soon as I stepped the first step I turned around and said, "What gifts do you guys have?" Alexia said, "Well, we can all speak out spells and Neptune is faster than anyone or thing whether he is running or walking. He can cause people pain as well but he is not as powerful as you it seems. I can change anyone's mind or any animals mind or thoughts. Trevor is very strong and can be invisible, and as far as me I can feel by touching or not whether it be love or hate or anger from any person. I stood their amazed and then finally said, "wow" they laughed but then said, "but you are more powerful then we are, we have searched for your gift and found that when developed the right way you can not only have visions and change them and read minds and feel the emotion inside the vision but you can protect a person in that vision as well as protect them in your mind by your thoughts and hopes and prayers. You can also cause pain by your mind or thoughts when you think of them and you don't have to say spells because as long as you think of it, it will happen. The last thing that you are capable of doing is that you can say spells from your mouth and mind as well as being able to move faster than Trevor here" I took all this in and was so overwhelmed but at the same time excited to learn this all. Trevor took my hand and led me up the stairs but as I got half way up Alexia said, "Oh Michelle, by the way Our brother has seemed to really like you so please don't hurt him because we wouldn't want it to result in a war" I stopped short and looked at Trevor as he blushed and then I said to him and the rest, "I have a boyfriend and I didn't realize that he was crushing on me, I thought he was just trying to be nice I'm sorry" Alexia and Neptune looked at Trevor and then said, "Trevor maybe you should not get to close to her if she feels that she will leave soon" Trevor grunted and said, "I don't care

I like her and I would fight for her If I need too" I blushed bright red because that is what Charley said in my vision and then I let go of his hand and said, "Trevor, I don't think that it is a good idea to fall for me because I know that my boyfriend will be here and come and get me and I love him so please I don't want to hurt you" He laughed and said, "This boyfriend of yours that you so love would fight for you too I am sure and yet he is not here nor did he try and stop you when you left, he is not worth it and I will fight him and win" I started to shake because I knew that this was true because I could see his thoughts and feel his heart beating faster and faster. I shut my mouth and walked out the door right past him and headed for the front door, He was right behind me and I didn't look around to face him, I just kept walking and then finally after a couple of minutes of silence he said, "Look, Michelle I promise that I will not hurt him or stop you if you leave, if this is what you want" I turned around and said, "I don't want you to hurt him or stop me because I want to be with him and only him, Trevor I need you to understand I have been through a lot and I have lost a love that I had a long time ago and when I met Charley he saved me from it and helped me through it and so I owe him more than my life and so please just leave me be" He frowned and then said, "your wish is my command" we walked down the road and he was showing me the best places to go and eat at as well as the places not to go and that bad things could happen there and until I was in control over my gifts that I should never go there by myself. I nodded at this and then we kept walking and then he took me to this old beat up field that looked like it was a baseball field once that was pretty far from the house and then he said, "Okay let's see what you can do?" I said, "Excuse me" He squatted down in a run position and then said, "Let's see your powers" I went to hesitate but then he shot past me and hit me in the back, and it was amazing how fast he was because I couldn't even see him but it happened so fast that I didn't know he had started to run he was so fast. I just stood there and realized that I was very different from them because I could control my spells and orders from my body and mind that is how I worked and how talented I am and the way I liked to work was by the mind and to bring pain to those who deserved it and so before I knew it I saw him and he was coming back around and pushed me and then anger started to come over me and I struck out not knowing what was really coming out and he went flying and hit the ground with a thud and didn't move. I stood there scared and then he got up and looked at me with shock and then said, "damn that was unexpected" But then he came at me and within a instant I felt his thoughts and so I decided to test it out more and when I reached his thoughts I brought pain to him more then I had done to anyone and then I saw him fall and hold his body like the little girl and soon he was hugging the ground and before I knew it I realized that I was about to kill him and so I let him go and he laid there for a while before he got up and looked at me and then he said, "You were going to kill me if you hadn't realized what you were doing huh?" She nodded and then said, "Sorry, I haven't been able to control it or be aware of it yet but it is in progress" He nodded and then said, "Okay, let's try something different and again except use a different tool. He started to come after me and this time I felt my protector that was mine around me and then I let it with my thoughts and body and sent him flying again into the air. The only thing that was different from the first time was that this time I had to focus and think with my thoughts the other time I didn't have too. Which I did not understand, but as he got up again and came at me again I was in the middle of thought so he came around me and struck me again and this time I landed hard on the ground and then when I tried to get back up he hit me again and this time it felt like a powerful hate cover me and I sprung up and hit him with all the hate and force I had and it hit him harder than before and this time he went flying and hit a tree about a mile away.

My New World. . . . . .

I couldn't believe this power and yet I didn't know where it came from either, I had known that even with the small amount that I had learned about it and the little that I have done with it but as he tested me I saw that I was able to do more and feel more when I was either attacking or protecting myself. It shocked me that after what I just did he came back walking tall and said, "Okay I am done, I won't test you no more tonight" I laughed and realized that I was having fun and then he laughed with me and then he said, " You know I think that you are more powerful then my brother and sister think and also I think that when you get mad or angry that your power goes into full force to protect you or whomever you want it to and your visions are separate from this gift". I nodded and said, "I agree with you" We smiled at each other and then kept walking until he brought me to this cliff and over the cliff was a river and we sat down and then I felt a tight feeling cover me and then I started to move forward and almost fell off the cliff when Trevor caught me and all I saw was black and then I saw Charley walking down the highway heading toward where I was and calculated that he will be here in a week and then as I saw his thoughts I could see and feel that he was scared and also full of fear that something bad happened to me and then I couldn't help myself and so I said to him that I was safe and training for my gifts and that I was in Atlanta, Georgia. In my vision he stopped as he read his thoughts and then said "really well I am on my way baby we need to talk this out, I love you" I smiled and then said,

"I know Charley and I love you too" The vision went black and then I came back and Trevor was holding me and saying " He can't have you, I have been looking so long for someone like you and I am prepared to die for you " I realized that he was holding me and then I stood up and pulled away and then said, "let's go back" He stood up reluctantly and then we walked back to his house in nothing but silence.

The whole way back I was thinking that I was crazy to walk out of his house not knowing where I was going to go and to be on my own but I was so angry that he would leave me behind. But he didn't he stayed and now he is coming for me and I will go with him, I think.......

I moved my head back and forth and tried to make sense of everything that I have found out and learned in the past couple of hours. As I walked with Trevor right beside me I could see why a girl would fall for him he was tall and good looking but at the same time he had this feeling that wrapped around him of pain, and danger that I found myself going toward him and this was not good. I had never been the type that went for dangerous ones but for some reason Trevor made me feel like I was special and he made me feel like I was a part of his world and that I should be But I knew that it was a phase and so I just kept walking and when we reached his house I was tired and relieved and so I crashed on his bed while he went and talked to his brother and sister about me I was sure but I didn't care. When he came back he grabbed a pillow and blanket and lies down on the floor and fell asleep. I stayed awake for a little bit and then said, "So, are they pleased or worried?" Trevor stood up and looked up at me and said, "well, they are surprised but are happy and they still want you to join us" I smiled a sly smile and said, "well, I'll think about it but my boyfriend is on his way to get me and I already have made up my mind to leave with him and be with him and my family" He frowned and then said, "we will see" Then he laid back down and then I heard silence and so I slowly drifted off to sleep worrying about what would happen when Charley came to rescue me. When I woke up I felt this strange feeling cover me and so I knew that it would be a very interesting day. Trevor was sitting next to me on the bed and was watching me and so when I opened my eyes

I saw him and said, "Can I help you?" He laughed and said, "Good Morning to you too" He kept watching me and then he leaned down and kissed me on the lips without me knowing at all what he was going to do and with this the only thing I could do was slap him when he finished. He looked at me and said, "What was that for?" I said, "I told you I was with someone and that was not right to do that to me without me saying it is okay" He looked at me and then said, "But last night you kept saying my name in your sleep so I thought it was right" I looked at him in shock and I said, "I did what?" He smiled and said, "yes, The whole night I heard you say my name and a guy named Charley and we were fighting for you and you kept saying Trevor help me" My mind was racing and found that what he heard was my dream of them fighting for me and in my dream I had chosen Trevor over Charley. I couldn't believe it and so for that I deserved it and so I said, "well, don't do it again unless you ask" He smiled and then said, "May I kiss you again my dear Michelle" I didn't know what to say or do and so I said, "whatever" I regretted it believe me because when he kissed me the second time everything that I felt for Charley and anything else disappeared and it was the best feeling ever but at the same time the worst. Almost like he took all of my emotions and worries and stress and was carrying them on his back and body instead of me carrying them and my body felt lifted and relaxed and it was the best feeling ever but I noticed that he didn't just take the feelings that I had for Charley but the ones I had for Timmy as well. It felt very strange and almost refreshing at the same time, but then I realized that it could have been a part of his plan or power to make me want him and to forget what I had or what I used to have and so I had to shake it off and not let it get to me or let it take over but I also knew then that I was in trouble and what I mean is big trouble. Because I can't fall for Trevor while being in love with Charley and still be fighting the feelings that I had for Timmy that caused me more pain then all of it. But I knew that with Timmy it was something that happened and that the love I had now would never die and so Charley would always be there for me as I would him and the love was real not something that Trevor could change. I found myself in a situation because even though I loved Charley my mind and body wanted to know Trevor more and so I had never felt anything like this for anyone and so now that I had Charley and fell for him and then now Trevor it was going to be hard to fix this one. I loved Charley because he was mine and believed in me as well as helped me through my hard times when that man hurt me and Timmy left me but now I had met Trevor and he was like me and knew about me and what I could do and knows my gift and his family as well. Trevor could teach me and I know that he would be there for me as well, but there was something about him that made me uncomfortable almost like he always wants control over his life and everything around him and for me that was not something I could live with. So, I am torn because they are both what I want and were looking for. I guess we will have to see what happens and where I belong, but as I was thinking this I realized that two days from today was the day that it will come to an end and then my body started to shake and I was scared for both of their lives. Trevor was watching me and then I realized that he was holding me and trying to make me feel better like he knew what was going through my head. I couldn't do anything because I felt like my world was falling apart and so the feel of his soft skin and strong hold made me just want to curl closer to him. After a couple of minutes I released myself and pulled myself together and then he finally let go and said, "I will not let him take the one person that I have ever cared for" I smiled and then frowned and said, "I'm sorry Trevor but in the end it is my choice not yours and I think that you need to let me decide please" He hesitated and then said, "Anything for you my love" I got up out of bed and got dressed and then me and Trevor walked to our hiding place and practiced my gifts and powers and this time it was amazing I not only made him fly over 10 yards but I was able to take the energy from me with my mind and emotions to control where I sent him and could either let him go and watch him flying in the air or not let go and watch him act like a puppet under my fingers. I didn't realize I was letting it get to my head until Trevor was trying to fight me and let him down but he and I both knew that it was not going to happen. But I let him go and for some reason I think I upset him because when I let him go and he went flying into a tree. Within a couple of seconds he hit the ground, jumped up in rapid speed and then went racing toward me before I could do anything he had knocked me to the ground and was on top of me pinning me to the ground. I wasn't scared and neither was he but I could see in his eyes that I had hurt his ego and I busted up laughing and then after a couple of seconds he was too. He leaned down and kissed me and my mind was racing in all kinds of directions but at the same time I was happy. He made me feel free and didn't tell me what to do or try and change my choices he just stood there in the shadow and watched me and protected me. My first thought of him a couple hours were that he wanted or liked control but I saw that with him and the way he acted with me was that he let me be me as Charley would even though I felt better about myself and soon after a week and Charley never showed yet my mind and body started to change for Trevor. I started to want him and want to be with him and never leave his side and I found that he didn't leave mine and it was the best feeling ever. After we were done we went back to the house and ate dinner and then went to bed and this time I told Trevor, "Trevor you can sleep next to me if you want but don't get any ideas" He smiled and then said, "I would never do that without you wanting too" He laid down and crossed his arms above his head and gazed at the ceiling while I did the same. He turned to me and said; "Darling, you should get some sleep" I laughed and said, "Why aren't you?" He smiled and then frowned and said; "Because I have a lot of thinking to do and preparing as well" I propped my body up on my arm and said, "Like what?" He said without looking at me and smiling, "Charley will be here tomorrow and I need to get ready for the fight I am willing to do for you, as well as the fight for my family." I stopped shaking and said, "How do you know?" He smiled at this and said, "Because I saw him and he is going to try and kill us but I hate to tell you this but he won't win." I sighed and then said, "Well, I will worry about my choice tomorrow I guess" He kissed me and said, "Yes, worry about tomorrow and just get some sleep" I fell asleep as he drew me closer to him and I laid my head on his chest. When I woke up I was not ready for this at all. I sucked it up and walked downstairs after getting dressed and showered and ate my breakfast with everyone. Then we went outside and waited for him to show up. He appeared around the corner at 12:00pm and it was the strangest feeling I have ever encountered because for the first time I didn't want to be a part of him or be with him. But I stood there in silence and when he saw me he smiled and so did I. I waited until he got on the porch and then from there it began. Trevor walked in front of me guarding me from Charley, his brother and sister walked behind me in a line. Charley stopped at the second step and walked backwards, Trevor glared at him and said, "You will not be taking Her nowhere, she is mine" Charley's face grew red and his dog like face started to show and he said, "I don't think so, witch she will always be mine and she is coming home with me" I stood frozen because I didn't know what to do or say, But then I got an idea and when I realized that they were yelling at each other and not paying attention to me, I slid past them all without them knowing I was gone and as soon as I jumped over the rails of the porch and hit the dirt I went running and faster than Charley had ever seen me or Trevor and I was testing them and they didn't even know it. I never once looked to see if they were following me I just kept running. I came to a tree that was hidden pretty good and then ran up it all the way to the top and sat on the branch and looked over to the house and could see them still yelling at each other and then Trevor stopped and turned around to see that I was not there. He took off at a run and hit the dirt like me and then headed in my direction, while Charley headed in the opposite direction. He went around the house and back and then started to head the same way as Trevor. Trevor never stopped, he just kept running and Charley would stop, smell, and then run again. It took them over 15 minutes but to my surprise Trevor found me first and he ran up the tree and stopped dead in his tracks when he saw my huge smile. He started laughing but then got serious and said, "Don't do that again, you scared me to death" I laughed and said, "I'm sorry but I had to test you guys and try and make my decision" He looked at me and then said, "Oh yeah, what will be my dear?" While we were talking Charley was on the foot of the tree and he was getting madder and madder as he saw Trevor kiss me and help me down the tree. When I reached the ground, I saw that his brother and sister came to view and when they reached us I sighed and said, "I am staying here for as long as I can" Everyone Cheered except Charley. I looked at him and said, "Charley I am sorry but maybe a week ago I would have left with you but I have found that I am one of them and always will be and I have also found that I love Trevor, I don't love you no more so please leave." I thought Charley was going to fight back and try and make me go home, but after I said those words he turned around and walked away with his back to me never looking back. I wanted to run after him, and after a few seconds I did, I yelled "Charley" He stopped and but didn't turn around. With shock he said, "What do you want Michelle, I have saved you from so many things, I have given you my heart when no one else could have it, I have been there for you no matter what and this is what I get in return?" in the meanest words I have ever heard come out of him. I stopped and hit the ground on my knees and started crying. He shut up and ran to me on the ground and holding me, I buried my head and face into him and he kept trying to calm me down.

The Hardest Thing to do. . . . . .

I looked up at him, I said, "Charley I love you I need you to know this, but I also have feelings for Trevor and I am like them more then you will ever know, I feel like this is where I need to be." He looked at me and then he said, "I understand but what you said to me was the worst thing I have had happen to me I think that you should be where you are happy and so if that means here then so be it I will leave and you will never see me again" I started to cry again and then I said, "But I want to be with you and him" He frowned and then said, "You can't have it that way, you are going to have to choose" He saw my face and said, "I'll tell you what I will stay outside in the woods tonight and by morning I will ask you for your decision and then we will go from there. I nodded and then when I turned around Trevor was behind me as well as his family. I turned to him and said, "Trevor tonight I am going to camp out in the woods far way from here and clear my head and make sure that this choice is what I want" He was confused and then grew mad and was like "Darling you aren't staying out here by yourself without protection, there are strange things that happen in these trees" I said, "I'm sorry but I need my space and peace, I will be back and you will all know my choice." I walked back to the house and walked in and grabbed blankets, food, water and clothes and then walked back out and entered the forest without looking back and seeing them looking back at me but I just kept walking North until I was about a 3 miles away from everyone. I set up camp and put down the blanket and found some fire wood and made a fire and then sat down on the log that was near the fire and closed my eyes. Without hesitation my mind went swirling and before I knew it everything went black and I could see Trevor and Charley fighting a couple of years ahead and in this vision I was more beautiful than ever imagined and in this vision I was more like Trevor then Charley but what I saw was that I had chosen Trevor over Charley. I could not believe that I would do that but in my heart I knew why and it was because their world was mine as well and I found that in my vision it was also how it was going to end and this was alarming but I knew that with my gifts I could not control destiny but accept it. I slowly came out of the vision with confusion on my face because this did not help me at all, but I sat there by the fire staring into it and thinking really hard of the positives and negatives to each side. When I realized that the sun had gone down and had come back up I was still sitting there with the fire slowly dying and had found that I still hadn't made up my mind yet. I fell asleep after not sleeping the whole night and when I woke up it was noon and so I got over 8 hours or sleep since I woke up before and then without warning or anything everything went black and another vision came into few and then I saw Trevor talking to his sister and brother and telling them that he had put a spell on me so that I would be with him and he made me have a vision of me and him married and me choosing him over Charley and this started to make me mad but I kept calm and soon after the vision went away. I got up and grabbed my stuff and walked back to the house with my head going in all kinds of directions. When I reached the white porch, I stopped and pushed the door open and saw that they were sitting at the table eating and I was so angry that I couldn't control it. I started yelling at them and even though the brother and sister didn't know until that moment I yelled at them as well and soon I turned to Trevor and said, "I don't know you thought you were doing but making me love you and want to be with you is the lowest thing a person could do, and so I have decided that I would never be with you for anything" I stormed up the stairs and grabbed the rest of my stuff and then headed back down and walked out the front door and went looking for Charley. I didn't have to look far because when I looked up and

I saw Charley walking to the house from the tree that was at the side of the house where he was staying. He came up on the porch and soon I realized that they were standing behind me but no one noticed him at all. They were all watching me and my face as well as my expression. After everyone was done I sighed and said, "Last night I had a vision that this family and Charley were fighting for something that was not real because Trevor tricked me and in this vision I was not with Charley but with the family, I find this difficult because I love you Charley and always will and so I took a deep breath and then said, "I have made up my mind and that is to leave with Charley and be with him." Trevor glared at me and Charley and so did his family. Charley smiled and then took my hand and guided me from the porch and I had my things already so we walked off the porch and then headed into the morning on our journey back home. I remembered that before when I went to get my things that I found a small ring on top of my folded clothes and there was a letter that said,

"Darling Michelle,

I don't know how to say this or who you will chose but I want you to be my wife. So, without further a due will you marry me? You don't have to say anything I will know when you put on the ring that your answer is yes." Love, Trevor

I sighed and wanted to put the ring on so badly but knew that I couldn't put it on. Instead, I wrote a note under his and it read:

"Dear Trevor,

I know that this is hard for you, but I need you to understand that Charley was there for me when a man hurt me and when the love of my life left me and forgot me and he was the first person that I ever fell in love with afterwards and he will always be my first and Charley also asked me to marry him in his own words but I know that you will find someone better than me and when you do, you will see. Goodbye Trevor"

I walked away when I was done and then walked out the front door and Charley grabbed my hand and I said bye to everyone and then we left down the road and to the left where our home was. We never looked back and we just walked and walked which seemed like forever. After the first or second day I looked at Charley and he looked back at me and I said, "Charley I don't think this is over at all, I think that we will come face to face with them again" He smirked and said, "I know we will, but that is okay because as long as I have the love of my life fighting by my side, I don't care" At the sound of this the vision came back to memory and with this I frowned and started to tear up, but stopped myself before Charley saw me. I knew that in the end I and he were not going to be together or so I thought until I found out that it was all a lie and that I could have Charley forever and ever and I was happy starting to prepare myself for this. As we walked in silence a thought occurred to me, I turned to Charley and said, "Charley why did you not take my car or yours to get here?" He laughed and said, "Why didn't you?" I laughed and said, "Good point!" Then I turned to him and said, "So, what did you learn about yourself?" He laughed at my wording and then said, "It's a long story, and you sure you want to know?" I glared at him and he laughed and he said, "Okay, Okay?" Then he sighed and said, "Well, Michelle It all began when I was a small kid, a mad scientist named Frank Smith, he was an older man about 65 and was very smart and he had this man take these kids when they were babies or small kids and we were all sent to this warehouse that was in the middle of nowhere and was dark and had rats everywhere and the walls were falling apart as well as the beds that were on the floor, the food was small portions and we had to use buckets to go to the bathroom. It was like we were slaves to this man and he cared only of his experiments. If he injected someone with his new DNA animal test and something bad happened then he would kill the kid or dispose of him or her. If he made progress and everything went okay then he would keep the boy or girl in a small room and record the changes and what they could do or what they couldn't do. It was really bad and hard to watch but we all had to and there we were put into these rooms and maybe two or three in each room, then he would have this lab that was filled with tubes and they were filled with this gene that he had created and tested to see how humans would mutate to it and then he began to inject each of us and study us and record the results and some died from it because their body couldn't take it and some grew strong and formed into these wolves and some husky's and some other animals and when we got the chance we all got together and attacked the scientist and killed him and destroyed the warehouse of evidence and tried to get on with our lives. He was a crazy old man and really thought that he could develop a new species and he trained us and after we got rid of him it was all we knew and we had to stick together but eventually we found our families and it was strange but they let me come home and I was so happy that I was safe and sound but they didn't believe me about the mad scientist and so they will never know." He paused and then said, "I asked my parents what happened to me but they tried to tell me about something else but it wasn't what I needed and so I went to one of my other friends that was like me and he told me and I found out that this started to develop a couple years back but all my friends that were with me developed at the same time and we are a pack and we do what we need to do when the time is right. But I never remembered what I was and how I became it either." But I also don't remember it all is because when you change the instincts and feelings and emotions that are filling your blood from the gene takes your memories and you forget some but gain some at the same time. But I fought this for a long time until a couple of years ago when it took over and I accepted it and took the change and I am still trying to control it but I realized when you left that loosing you was not going to happen and that I would rather have you and fight this then to not have you and live forever without aging or growing and not having you in my life." He paused and then said, "also I learned later that this gift or curse whichever you want to call it is very different and strange and what I mean is that I can change only change into a Husky dog, but I don't age or dye and I see and feel emotions and what people think as well as I see and feel like the dog its self. I walked by him not saying a word thinking that he was not done, then I realized that he was done and so I turned to him and said, "Charley I want to say that I will be forever with you, I do love you and will be here for as long as I can and my life will allow me" He looked at me funny and then said, "You had a vision of you being with Trevor in a couple of years didn't you, but he altered it and it is making you confused and mad huh?" I nodded and then said, "I thought that what I was feeling was real and then I realized that he was tricking me and that the only person that has ever loved me and wanted me and stood by me was the one that I was going to let go and so I feel that he deserves to be punished for it but I also feel that we will not hear the end of him either. I stopped and looked at him like how did he know. He bent his head back and laughed and then said, "Wow, Michelle do you really think that your visions are always 100 percent correct?" I glared and said, "They haven't lied to me yet" He Laughed again and said, "We will see" I kept glaring at him from the corner of my eyes and kept walking and then with shock he grabbed my arm and dragged me into the woods, when we reached there I stopped and said, "what are you doing?" He said, "I want to change so that it is easier and faster to get home" I said, "Oh" Then I said, "Are you going to carry me?" He laughed and then said, "Unless you want to fly?" For a second I forgot what I was and then I said, "You know what I will race you home" We laughed and then I kicked my feet and like I was a bull ready to go forward and then I got my mind ready and thoughts and before he could start to take off I was half way down the forest running and flying at the same time trying to get as far away and to beat him. I looked behind me and saw that he was nowhere near me and then I saw him running to my left about 2 or 3 miles out trying to catch up. I laughed out loud and in the distance I could hear him growl under his breath and it made me laugh even harder. We kept running and flying and when we reached his house a couple days later I was the first one there but he was right at my heels so it was a tie and then we went up to his room and sat on his bed to catch our breath. Before I could do anything he leaned down and took my face into his hands and kissed me and within that moment nothing mattered and in that moment I realized why I fell in love with him. I didn't want him to stop and for a long time he didn't he just kept kissing me, I stopped him after a couple of minutes and said, "What about my parents?" He pulled back and then he said, "Don't worry I called them and told them I was bringing you home and they said they want to talk to you but you are allowed to stay here as long as you want." I waited and then he said, "My parents made a room for you next door and said, that you can move in whenever you are ready. My eyes got big and then I said, "REALLY" He laughed and said, "Yes, my love you are mine forever" I laughed and said, "Well, Duh my silly Charley."

A New Start. . ..

My mind was racing because I never even dreamed that my parents would let me live with Charley or his parents for that matter since I have never met them. But I knew that this was the time to make everything right that I did and caused my parents for leaving and so without further a due I called my father and after a couple of rings he answered the phone and said, "Hi Michelle, your mother and I are very glad that you came back and even though we should ask why you left we feel that it was your choice for some reason and so we are just going to say that you are old enough to make your decisions but we hope that next time you will tell us and confide in us." He paused and this gave me the freedom to say something and so I said, "Dad, I'm sorry that I left without telling you and I promise that if I decide to go the road that the world takes me that I will tell you both before I go, I also wanted to say that I love you both and am glad that you trust me and Charley enough to let me stay with him." I stopped and my father said, "Yes, my dear we do and we hope that you both live your life the best way that you can because you are only young once, just keep in touch with us and you can come home at anytime." I smiled and said, "Thanks dad I love you." He smiled and said, "Your welcome honey and we love you too." He hung up and when I closed my cell phone, Charley was standing next to me. I looked up at him and he said, "Everything okay?" I smirked and said, "Yeah, a little too easy" Charley laughed and said, "Well, what you want to do now?" I laughed and said, "I don't know what can we do?" He laughed and then said, "Anything you want?" I said, "Okay, well I need some things from my house if you don't mind?" He nodded and then said, "What do you need babe?" I looked at him and said, "As much as you can bring?" He nodded and said, "Okay, I will take my car and get as much as I can and then we can go tomorrow and get the rest okay dear?" I said, "Okay" and then he was gone and for the first time I felt alone and it was scary because the last time I had a vision that I thought would be real or come true scared me. But I stood up straight and stood up and walked down stairs and started making dinner for the man that I loved. After 30 minutes he came back into the house through the front door carrying my stuff up to my room. When he came back down the stairs and was calling my name and realized that I hadn't answered him he panicked and found me in the kitchen with dinner on the counter all ready but I was standing there with a spoon in my hand and was frozen stiff as the world grew black and everything was wrong and full of pain and through this world I could see Trevor and his family growing and making plans to fight, but in this world it was years in the future because I was with Trevor and not charley and then I saw me and Charley on the opposites sides and we were both dying a little as the fight progressed. After a couple of minutes the vision stopped and I came back to reality and when I opened my eyes I was on the floor with Charley beside me holding me and the first time he was crying. I slowly touched his hair and he turned to me and then without warning he pressed his lips to mine and said, "Please, I can't lose you again it is the worst feeling ever, if you only knew what it does to me." I put my finger to his lips and said, "Shhhh... I'm not going anywhere, I promise." He kissed me again and then helped me up from the floor and then helped me set out the food and then we ate by the television and watched something funny but romantic. The whole time he was running his hands through my hair as I laid my head down on his lap and for the first time in a while I was happy and Trevor was just a memory and then it hit me that maybe Trevor was just someone that I wanted because I could not really have him. With this it made me feel better after this and then I started to cuddle closer to Charley and he caught on to my passion and unexpectedly he didn't stop me. I slowly got up and wrapped my legs around him to straddle him on the couch so that I could see his face and his eyes told me that he was scared but full of love as well. I leaned down and kissed him, then he kissed me back and said, "God, baby I have missed you so much" I smiled and then placed my hands on his face and said, "Charley you have no idea how much I missed you and love you" I took a deep breath and then I said, "I was also scared that you wouldn't come after me and get me" He looked at me shocked and then said, "Why would you think that ever?" I said, "Well, you never followed me" He looked down and then said, "Honestly, I thought you were going for a walk to cool off and then when it was dark and then the next day I realized that you were gone forever and each day I died a little and then after talking to my parents and the others like me, we set out to find you" I looked down at him and said, "Charley, I'm so sorry I didn't mean to hurt you." He smiled and said, "No, you were right, I should never have even had considered leaving you behind when you are my everything, and so now I make a promise to you my Michelle." He stopped and then said, "I promise to never leave you again, to love you forever and all eternity, to be devoted to you, to be true to you, to be honest and be there for you no matter what." I smiled and then said, "I promise you my heart, mind, body, and soul, I will love you forever and always, I promise to never leave you ever again, to be true to you, to be honest, and to be there for you no matter what" We kissed again and I unwrapped my legs from around him and then laid back down and he played with my hair again and kept kissing my neck. I looked up at him and a question popped into my head and what came out was, "Charley, what did you mean by others?" He smiled and said, "I was hoping you would ask" then he said, "well, there are more out there that are like me and different people so all I have to do is send out the word and they will be here if I need them" I said, "So, they were there when you came to get me?" He laughed and said, "yes, but they were far away unless I needed them" I smiled and said, "Wow, your good" He laughed even harder at this and said, "I told you, you are my everything I would die for." I looked at him very serious looking and said, "Over my dead body" He got serious and then said,

"This is not up to debate at all" I laughed and said, "We will see" He glared at me but turned his head back to the TV. and continued to play with my hair and kiss me. The next thing I knew I was asleep on his lap relaxed and happier then I have ever been. I never thought that my feelings for Charley would go away but for some reason I felt so sure that I wanted him and he wanted me and so because of this I knew in my heart that Trevor tricked me and tricked my visions and I know that if he wanted to he could do it again and I knew now that he was just a phase or someone that I had desired at the time before I found out that he was someone that I could never be with or ever want but my love will never change for Charley and so I have found that even though my visions say that Trevor is the one that I am suppose to be with I will fight and fight to be with Charley because no one will ever be able to do what he has for me. I looked up at him and he was watching my face wondering what I was thinking, I smiled and then kissed his hand and then turned my face to the TV. and when I did this he softly turned my face back to him and said, "What are you thinking?" I smiled and said, "Nothing important" He looked at me and said, and "I don't believe you "I sighed and then said," Okay, promise me you won't get mad at me He looked at me and said, " I promise" I sighed again and then said, "Well, I was trying to figure out why he would do something like that to make me want him or love him, also even though at that time when he tricked me and I fell for Trevor so fast and then went through all of my visions and they all say that in the end I will be with him but I have decided that no matter what I will fight and fight to be with you because no one can ever be there for me or love me like you and that is all I want is you" When I stopped his face changed and he became bitter and then he looked down at me and said, " I know that you think that I left you and or abandoned you but I need you to know something, the day that you thought I was going to leave you and when you said those words to me it made me reconsider and I was going to take you with me but at a distant just in case it was going to be dangerous and then my parents came home and told me the story and I kept trying to track you and find you but realized that you weren't anywhere near home and that's when I heard you in my thoughts when I was traveling and trying to find you that way, but I need to you know that I wouldn't have stopped until I found you because I love you and I would never do anything to hurt you." I sighed and then I said, "I'm sorry my love and I know how stupid it was now and I promise that I will never do it again and that I will never hurt you either and I can understand if you are mad at me and don't want me either." He looked at me with pain and anger and said, "Michelle have you not heard a word I said, I love you and would do anything for you, I'm not mad at you I'm mad at him and I know that you are not going anywhere nether am I" I looked into his eyes and said, "I love you Charley more then you will ever know" I realized at that moment that I didn't tell him about Timmy and seeing him and so I sighed and said, "Charley I have to tell you something, I need you to be calm and not get upset." He looked at her and was studying her face and when he saw that she was feeling guilty he knew that it was something not good and so he tried to relax and then he said, "Okay" Then she sighed again and said, "Well, when I was walking in Atlanta, Georgia I came across Timmy the guy that I fell in love with before and found that he was with someone that he didn't want to be and that she was bad and her father was the head of a mob and I tried to tell him that I couldn't help him and I told her that if she ever hurt him or his family I would kill her and she laughed at me and so I had to show her and I caused her pain and almost killed her." She stopped and then said, "He tried to get me to stay but I didn't I left him and then met Trevor but nothing else happened and sometimes I wished that I should have stayed and made sure that he was okay and his family but I know that it is something that he has to deal with". He kept looking at her and then he said, "Well, I can understand that, but it is like you said he has to deal with it and so don't worry about it" She tried to read his face but couldn't see anything. She finally said, "Are you mad at me?" He looked at her and said, "did anything else happen?" She watched him and then said, "He tried to kiss me but I pulled him and off" He saw that she was telling the truth and then he said, "Then no, I have no reason to be mad" She relaxed and then He looked right back at me and said, "I love you my Michelle and I trust you and so there is nothing to worry about but I have something for you" I jumped up and said, "You didn't?" He smiled and said, "Wait here?" He went to his room and came back down holding a little black box and when he came back he knelt down before me and said, "Michelle, I know that we have a life time to know each other and that you are scared for this but I love you and I will do anything for you and be there for you forever and always, and so with this will you marry me?:" After he said those beautiful words he opened the box and inside was 10kt gold ring with white and sapphire diamonds all along it and a gold band to match it as well. I looked at the ring and then at him and the words could not even come out right because what I said was "Charley, you know that I'm not the type to go this far especially when we have not been together for that long" I saw his face sadden and it made me hurt inside and before I could speak he got up and took it back to his room. Before he got to the stairs I said, "Charley, I wasn't done I love you with all of my heart and I have found out in the time that we have shared and had that I don't want to be with anyone but you and my heart only belongs to you and so Yes I will marry you" He turned around and was smiling happily and then he picked me up and kissed me so passionately and hard that I pulled him closer and then he took the ring and put it on my finger. I looked at it and said, "wow, this is beautiful" He smiled and said, "I got it for you a while ago but I was waiting for the right moment and day for it but I wanted to know if you would be mine" I grabbed him again and said, "Of Course I would be yours Charley, you are everything to me and that will never change" He kissed me again and then we went back to the couch and laid down watching TV and then I slowly started to drift to sleep and before I was out completely I could feel Charley picking me up and carrying me upstairs to my room that was connected to his.

Unsure of the Unknown. . ..

The white house was dark with candles burning and in the small room that was cold and deserted from the day of family, except in the distance there in the recliner by a fire was Trevor reading the book of spells and pondering what spell to use for the love he lost. He finally came upon one and it read; "As the sun shines, the night calls out to the souls of those who had been taken, with this heart that craves for this lost one, bring her or him to the one that had lost it, by the power of the heart still beating and longing for it." Trevor smiled at this and knew that he was going to use it with every power that he could use to make sure that his Michelle was brought back to him no matter what means. He stood up and lit a few more candles and then held the book up right in front of him and as his brother and sister started to form behind him and agreed with his choice they slowly chanted this spell over and over again. When it was all done the candles went out and the curtains blew up from the wind that blew from outside and this is how they knew that it was done. Trevor smiled and looked at his brothers and sisters and said, "It is done now we wait and see what happens" They nodded at him in agreement and then his sister said, "Are you sure, you want to do this because you know what will happen" Trevor smiled a wicked smile and said, "Sister I have been waiting for someone like her for a while now and I will not lose her to this guy Charley, I will fight him until I kill him if I have too" They nodded and then they all left the room except Trevor and while he waited for his love and sat down on the couch and he dreamed of their life and how it would be as well as the love they would have and the kids that would come from it. He never thought that it would be easy but he knew that she would not know what was happening or remember because this spell would not be broken unless Charley killed him and that would never happen. Trevor smiled at this thought and then he sat further into the couch until the love of his life was in his arms.

Across the way in Charley's house, Michelle was sleeping and in the middle of the night her body was lifted from the bed and she floated over the bed in the air as her mind was controlled by the spell from Trevor and even though she could see her bed and where she was, she could not stop the power that was controlling her and before she knew it she was writing on a piece of paper that said;

Dear Charley, My beloved is mine and don't bother coming for her because I will fight for her till death so save yourself and live on with your life. Trevor.

Then Michelle floated out the window in the middle of the night in her pajama's and as the wind blew through her hair and the cold breeze felt good she was scared but at the same time trying to fight the power that was stopping her from being with Charley. She even tried to scream but for some reason the words would not come out and this made her even more scared. What seemed like forever ended finally and then she could see that she was in front of the white house that made her feel like home but at the same time she felt like what was there was trying to make her into something that was not what she wanted to be after all. She walked forcefully to the front steps and as the door swung open and Trevor stood there smiling she was forced to smile back. Trevor took her hand and helped her inside and then sat her down on the couch where the fire was burning and warming the house. He kissed her and she was forced to kiss him back, she was unhappy and he could tell. He wanted her to love him for him and by her will and heart not by force but he was afraid to let her free of the spell. He decided that he was going to keep her under the spell until he knew the time was right and then he might let her go of it. But instead he took her hand and then helped her upstairs and into his room where he changed his clothes and she did the same and they both crawled into bed at the same time. She fell asleep and he stayed awake and watched her as she slept and to make sure no one tried to take her from him. As she slept he could tell that she was dreaming of Charley and this hurt him but he could not change her dreams right now. So, he let them happen but he held her tighter as she dreamed and then kissed her forehead and then rested his head on the head board thinking of the life that they would have and how happy and free they will be. When morning came Trevor was so happy but when he looked at Michelle her face was pale and she looked different then she did the night before, he looked at her and said, "What is happening to you?" She looked at him and finally was able to say, "What do you mean?" She got up and looked in the mirror and saw that her beauty was fading and her heart was empty and she was slowly changing into someone that was ugly and that looked dead. Trevor horrified got up and went over to her and said, "What have I done to you?" She turned around and said, "You took me away from the love of my life and the one person that has me completely and the longer you keep me here the faster I die." Trevor was mad and yet excited because this meant to him that if Charley didn't save her fast enough then no one could have her." Michelle heard Trevor's thoughts and with an instant she slapped him across the face and said, "You would let me die so that Charley could not have me, which is not love that is just jealousy as well as stupid." Trevor laughed and said, "We will see my love" Michelle glared at him and said, "I am not yours nor am I your love, I never was and I never will be" Trevor smiled and said, "We will see" Michelle got frustrated and walked away, and then with the best power that she had she concentrated really hard and within a couple of seconds she was inside of Charley's mind and she said, "My Darling Charley, I need you to wake up and go to my bedroom and you will find a letter that I was forced to write but I also need you to know that Trevor has kidnapped me and he has me under a spell that can only be broken by him or his family or if you kill him but I also need you to know that I am dying slowly and fast at the same time and I will not last long." She could see Charley jumping up from the bed and then he was reading the letter and within a couple of minutes he was dressed and out the door, then she heard him say "I'm going to kill him, I swear on my life I am going to kill him with my bare hands this time, I love you my darling Wife to be and I promise that I will not let you die because without you I am nothing and without you my life will follow you" She could hear him running and he paused and then he said, "Baby, I am going to get my crew together and I will be there faster than you could ever imagine, I love you and I am on my way" She smiled at this and then replied, "I love you too Charley and I will be waiting." She turned around to see Trevor watching her and then he grabbed her hand and fled down the stairs and called his brother and sister. They came from the kitchen and stopped when they saw Michelle, They pointed and then his sister said, "What did you do to her?" Trevor ignored her and said, "Listen to me, Charley is on his way with his army if you may it call it that and we need to be ready as well." His sister said "don't worry his friends won't touch us". Michelle was suddenly scared because she didn't know how many friends Charley knew but she knew that no matter what she would not let Trevor have her. She didn't want to die but she was going to have a plan of her own the best way that she could to make sure that he didn't have her.

Charley hurried to his friend Chad Richard's house and told him to tell everyone that this is important and that they need to get together ASAP and so within 30 minutes they were all at Chad's house and discussing the options that they had. They had over 20 kids that were like Charley and they all escaped the prison that they were stuck in because of Charley so they grew closer together and so Charley told them what was going on and they all agreed that it was time to teach these witches not to mess with them. His good friends Patrick Hexton, Brad Allen, Marvin kelmar and Chad hurried and made something for everyone to eat and then headed out the door toward the white house that held Charley's soon to be wife. They didn't know what they were getting into but at the same time they didn't care, they kept running and never stopped until they reached the back of the house. Charley told the boys to sit tight and then he walked around the house and saw that they were inside sitting around a table and eating dinner it looked like. Charley walked around back to his crew and then told them that they should attack now but he didn't know how yet. The boys started to spit out suggestions but the only one that sounded promising was burning the place down, he knew that he taking a chance but he was going to run in and pull Michelle out while they all burned. The boys found gasoline and spread it over the house, then Chad light a match and the house started to spark and soon flames were moving so fast that it was hard for Charley to get through the back door but he busted it down and then smelled for Michelle only to see that her sent had changed but still found her in her room trying to get out. He pulled her forward and she wrapped her arms weakly around his neck, when he reached the bottom again Trevor was standing there guarding the door with his sister and brother on each side of him. Charley growled and then started to walk forward not afraid, Trevor lifted up a piece of wood over Charley's head and was about to make it fall. Then he realized that she was on his back and so he stopped and then made it crash against the house as it was falling around them. Charley spoke very firmly and harsh and said, "You may kill the love of my life but you will never kill me and soon, I will come for you and kill you with my bare hands." Trevor laughed out of pure uncertainty and then without warning his skin began to disappear as he was on fire and within seconds and his screams he was no longer there. His brother and sister shocked and so they had no choice but to take the curse off of Michelle and when they did. Michelle regained her strength and was back to normal and was no longer under the spell. Charley smiled and kissed her in his dog form and she smacked him while wiping her mouth of dog drool but laughed out loud. They both laughed and then he walked past the brother and sister and ran through the woods with the rest of the boys. The brother and sister not sure what to do but at the same time they didn't want Charley to kill them and so they stepped aside and Charley told them "I will let you live if you leave us be but if I find out that you are near us or anything I will kill you" They nodded and then watched as Charley picked up Michelle and They ran faster than ever and ran until they got home, but this time Charley took her to their place of peace and they stayed there till the next morning. When she woke up she remembered that her grandfather and Uncle were coming down, she looked at Charley and saw that he was looking at her. She smiled and then said, "Charley where are my relatives?:" He smiled and said, "Oh yeah, I called them a couple of days ago and told them what happened and then told them that I was coming to save my wife to be and that they can still come if they wanted too." He paused and then said, "But they said no and that they will visit soon and to be safe and that they were really busy so I'm sure that we will see them soon" I sighed of relief and then said, "Charley baby, we need to go we have a wedding to plan" He laughed and then said, "You mean I have to help?" I laughed and then said, "Yes you are!" We laughed and then we walked to his car that was hidden in the bushes and we drove back to his house to dress and to sit down with his mother and my mother only she was not here because she was still in New York. But we planned the wedding the best without her, and we finally picked a date and it was set to be a year from this date which was August, 16th. I picked the maid of honors and their dresses out of a magazine and then his tuxedo with his best men and then we found a park and minister to do the marriage right and then our quests and catering.

Planning what was New to me. . ..

We had it all done and good within a couple of months and would have it paid off before that time as well. My father actually paid for it but his father wanted to help and so they split it and even though I felt bad about them having to pay for it all even though that was what it was suppose to be like. I finally let it go and then after going to school every day and keeping my grades up soon I knew that me and my Charley would be together forever and live a long healthy life. But as she thought this she knew that her fears not yet over.

After what had happened to her almost a year now she could feel her anger and hate for people and men to develop and so she knew that her world was going to change and before she could think another thought her phone rang and it was her Grandfather, but she was unsure if she could or should trust him and the Uncle that he claims but he told her things about her family that no one knew and so she believed him. He told her that if she wanted to know more about her life and to be able to deal with it and control it to meet him at the south side woods about 3 miles from her house. She agreed and then her grandfather Bernard Anderson and her Uncle Frank Stanford told her that to be there on Saturday at 9:00am. She told them no problem because she knew that her parents would be away that day and for the next month so it was no big deal. When she got off the phone with them she realized that Saturday was tomorrow and she was kind of nervous but at the same time excited. She finished what she was doing and then went to bed.

When she woke up the next morning she had a feeling that she was going to get dirty and so she ate breakfast and showered and dressed in her jogging outfit. She carried her music and food and water and clothes as well as everything else that was important. She walk into the woods not fearing anything, and even carrying her book bag that held everything she started to jog and then her speed picked up and before she knew it she was full speed and was running faster than any human could have imagined. It felt like a long time but within minutes she saw two men sitting around a burned out camp fire and so she told against the tree smug and watching as they were arguing about her. She laughed a loud and when they heard her they jumped and then realized that it was just her and laughed too. They told her to sit down and then started to tell her what they knew which was not much for her benefit anyway. They were part witches and part human so their blood was not as pure but as far as she knew neither was her's. But she knew that she was better and that the blood that flowed through her was stronger. Her grandfather after finishing told her of his past and how he was in the military to be a part of the secret organization and was to kill those that were supposed to be disposed but he was retired and her Uncle was the same just a different branch. She was amazed and wanted to learn more, she looked at them and said, "Can you teach me to be dangerous and strong?" They laughed and then said, "Yes, but you will have to understand that your powers are strong already and so we will have to help you control them, but it will take a long time but for now we will teach you the basics." She smiled in agreement and then they walked down into the woods where they set up a small training exercise and so he told her quickly what to do, which was crawl under wire that was a long tunnel, run up logs that were put together like a raft, jump down then run to a wall and climb over it, then grabbing rope and hitting the top of the wood, then back down and running in about 2 miles before being done. She was supposed to do it in 10 minutes if that and she was able to do it in like 9. She was mad but her grandfather and Uncle told her that with practice she will get better. She felt better and then kept at it for a long time, feeling her powers wanting to reach out and help her and makes her better but she wanted to do this on her own until the time was right. After many hours of work they all stopped and it was 5:00pm and so they ate dinner and slept around the camp fire until the next morning. When she went to sleep if felt like a wave of everything disappeared and that she finally understood what she suppose to be. Before she knew it she was being woken up by them and they were yelling at her, she jumped out of unconsciousness and found that they were standing over her. She jumped up and looked at them; their faces were worried and yet determined. They sighed and then lend her down a rocky road and when they reached a cliff they stopped gazing at the sun coming from the end of the world. She waited for them to saying anything but they remained silent and this bothered her. She took a deep breath and then opened her mouth to say something but before she could her grandfather turned and said, "We are going to do something harder today, you will not like it and you will be tired and probably quit but we need to test something." She just looked at them and then said, "Okay, let's go" they walked back into the woods and then her grandfather said, "You see that ribbon on the tree? You start there and then you keep running through the forest until you see a Red ribbon that is wrapped around two separate trees and then when you get there you will have a surprise but it is your job to go by instinct and do what your mind and heart tell you and then if you get past that you continue to run until you reach the tunnel and you are suppose to run through that as well, once you get to the other side you will see or hear something it is your job to do the right or wrong thing whichever is your choice. After you take care of that then you are to keep running until you are finished with the tasks and challenges." When he finished she was so beyond nervous but she knew that she was being tested and so she was ready and knew that running wouldn't make her tired so that was a plus. She went to the tree and waited for him to tell her when to start, then he blew the whistle and she took off faster than before and kept running and flying through the air and jumping from tree to tree never hitting the ground, at the same time she was gazing at every tree that passed by and finally after a few feet she saw the tree and when she landed on the ground and headed toward it. She realized the danger that was around her and knew her instinct was to kill with no questions or need for answers. Before she knew it a man in all black came up behind her and grabbed her behind the neck and tried to pull her down but to his surprise she didn't move and within seconds she took his arm breaking it with a snap and then flew him across the forest hitting a tree very hard. Before she had time to breath more came and soon she was fighting each one either two at a time or one and they kept coming. After a little while and she killed them all was when she could take a moment to breath and then she kept running until she came to the next task which was wild animals and poisonous snakes in which she jumped over and then she got to the tunnel and found her biggest fear which was a person in need and pain. She stopped not sure what to do but then realized that she would take them to the hospital but realized there was no time so she used her gift to fix the person that had a broken leg and then with her mind fix the person's image of what had happened and to him it was all a dream. He walked home unhurt and untold of the secrets she had, she ran under the tunnel and to the other side and back through the woods to find only a few feet a creature she had never seen before it was as tall as a bear but with the body of a human with a tail like a lion and this creature was a pure monster of all that she ever saw. She slowly moved toward him watching her movements and waiting for him to strike her but she realized that he was waiting for her. She didn't move and then he started to run toward her and she jumped over him landing hard on the dirt, he turned around coming after her again and this time he took his sword and struck at her but missed and before he could strike again she used her power with great force and struck him in the head, then the chest, and then the stomach and soon her strikes were like lighting coming from her and soon he fell to the ground like in slow motion, but with the force so big that he landed harder than ever but never got back up and so she was running faster than ever and the feeling that was coming over her never faded. The anger and power of destroying something so big made her feel bigger than she ever had before. She ran until she was in front of her Grandfather and Uncle again and they were congratulating her and cheering her on and so they celebrated for awhile. They told her that the next couple of weeks were going to be harder then today but they knew that she would make a great warrior. She stopped eating and looked up at them and said, "What?!" They both looked at her and then her grandfather said, "Michelle we are training you with our military background so that you can use your power however way you want, you have to choose whether for good or bad but we are just here to teach you what we know." She relaxed and then said, "right" She fell asleep and soon it felt like the next weeks were nothing but harder than her normal life and even though she had break from school for awhile she was starting to feel even stronger than before, her only worry was that the powers that she was using were not all that she could do but she knew that soon they will surface and so she trained hard, not trusting no one or loving anything but the woods, her fear and emotions became controlled and never exposed and soon at the end of the weeks she was a lethal weapon fighting with so many champions and those that have won so many times. Her grandfather and Uncle was so proud and soon after they left to go back to their homes she stayed in the forest for a couple of days trying to find the answers that she needed and keeping herself away from others until she could control her emotions and her powers and hate for those that hurt her. Also, knowing that she had to choose her life style and control it as well and how much time she had. She headed back home a few days later and waited until the next morning for school to start again before she exposed herself to others and she would have to live life the best that she could.

Another to save.. ..

After she got home she had a vision of a girl being mugged by the candy store a couple streets down from her house, she jumped up from the table and headed out the door faster than she expected and then ran toward the girl. When she got there the guy was hitting her and punching her with his fists and this made Michelle's anger and emotions surround her stronger than ever. She ran toward them with no fear and no feeling but to kill on contact. She ran up to the man and hit him with a blow that could have killed anyone, but he turned around and laughed out loud. She didn't stop but this time she went into his mind and made his worst nightmares come true and with this he laid on the ground in total horror and never moved or got up. Michelle then took all her power and strength and ended his life right in front of the girl that was cradling her legs and trying to hide. Michelle stopped and looked at the girl and with fear and hate in her eyes she saw that the girl could see this and so without saying anything to explain the girl ran away screaming. Michelle didn't care because she knew that she didn't look normal at all, she has long auburn hair that fell to her back with blue eyes that glistened in the night and a nose ring in her right nostril and long black earrings that dangled from her ears and two white pear like earrings in her cartilages above her ears as well. She was wearing her tight jeans that hugged her body and thighs as well as her hips and boots that were knee high and her shirt was blacker then the night and her makeup was bold with red and black eye liner bolder than ever. She knew that people would call her a freak but she only cared about helping others or destroying those that deserve it, not what people thought about her. Even though everyone at school was shocked with the change and were afraid of her she tried to hide her feelings and be nice as much as she could but it was hard for her. As she walked the streets at night seeking for something that made her happy or that would help her find the reason why she felt this way or the way she was anyway. She continued to walk the streets at night and one night she thought it would never end, she walked the streets and came across this group of guys that were taken advantage of a girl that looked like she was 16 and they had her pinned against a alleyway and even though the girl could not scream because she had duck tape across her mouth. Michelle grew angry with this and she took action harsher than ever and so she let the anger come over her and then after it had within her mind she thought of the actions that she wanted to do and the pain that she wanted to cause them. She thought okay for the first one his heart will stop beating, and soon the first guy she saw dropped backwards as his heart stopped beating. The others kept going tearing her clothes off and touching her while she stood kicking and hitting and helpless. Next Michelle thought the other two will have their genitals ripped off and no longer be able to have them back. And so within a couple of minutes the two guys she saw screamed in horror and was holding themselves as they began to be ripped apart from what they cherished and thrown to the ground. Michelle laughed but continued as she thought of one more for the last two, which was that they would be lifted up and thrown into the wall. After this act was done, the girl tried to cover herself and when Michelle walked over to her holding some extra clothes. The girl looked at her confused but Michelle smiled and said, "I'm sorry if I scared you but I couldn't stand there they and let them hurt you like that so I made sure that they got what they deserved." The girl kept looking at her and then said, "Thank you, but how did you do that?" Michelle laughed and said, "You wouldn't believe me if I told you, but I will walk you home if you like" The girl nodded and never asked any more questions, but got dressed quickly and then her and Michelle walked down the street and two blocks to her house. After Michelle knew she was safe, she walked away and into the night again. As she walked into the night she could hear the girl's thoughts that she just saved and smiled as she knew that she had made a new friend. She kept walking and soon not long after she turned the corner she saw a man coming out of a house with a little girl that was tied up and gagged, she didn't have to walk over because she knew that it would make it worse for the little girl and so what she did was take a deep breath and then closed her eyes and went into her mind and powers and searched for everyone that she could see and read and then found him seeing what he saw and what he said and then she spoke as if it was his own thoughts, and said return her before your life ends because the man that wants her will kill you even after you deliver her. She could see the man stop and realize this and then for some reason it worked and the man took her back and released her back to her family. The man got back into his truck and then drove off, Michelle knew that that was two easy but she waited and he never came back so she continued on walking and before she knew it was 4:00 am, she felt a lone since Charley and she had been busy. She knew that he hated it when she left home at night to fight the world of their monsters and she knew that he was still uneasy about the way she was now but it was who she was, She tried to make him understand but the words never came out right and even though she told him that they were a team she knew in her heart that this was something that she had to do on her own. Charley was gone the day that her grandpa and uncle turned her this way and helped her be who she was but she was glad because she felt another person inside of her almost evil and she didn't want Charley to see that. Michelle also knew that soon she would have Charley by her side killing those that took away from her and the world but for now she was enjoying the control and freedom and peace and quiet.

She was trying to sleep as she lay next to Charley but she kept going in and out of a vision that was trying to break through and she was fighting it, soon it came through and she could see Timmy standing by a bridge waiting for someone but there was no one there and he was sad and lonely. Then she saw him turn and there she saw herself walking toward him only to find that she didn't know what to feel or say but she kept walking to him knowing that deep down her love for him still remained, as she saw herself getting closer to him the visions slowly started to fade away and before she knew it Charley was shaking her and when she came back he was holding her and saying "Baby, it's okay I will fight for you until the end if it comes to that, you don't have to go to him if you don't want to." She then realized that she had been talking out loud to Timmy and that Charley heard her. She leaned into him and started kissing him everywhere and then she looked up at him and said, "Charley, I will always love him but I don't know if I would be able to just leave you and be with him, it hurts me to think about it but I know that one day it will come to me having to see how much I love him and how much I love him." Charley nodded in understanding and said, " I told you that I don't want you to feel compelled to be with me and that if you want to be with I will fight for you and try but I can't make you love me as much as him and so when the time comes we will deal with it then." I smiled and then hugged him close and said, "You are too good to me Charley and I couldn't have asked for anyone better then you, I love you Charley and that is all I need is you and knowing that you love me too" She saw him smile and then frown but he kissed her and hugged her close and then pushed her back to the bed and cuddled against her and soon they fell back to sleep. When she woke up she wanted to heal his scars knowing that he was hurting because she still loved someone that had hurt her and left her and went on with his life. She knew that one day she would find him or he would find her and then she would be in a bad situation but she also knew that for right now she was with Charley and when that day came then she would deal with it. She got up and looked over at Charley while he remained asleep, she thought it was funny because even after everything had happened her and Charley was not as intimate then her and Timmy was but she liked it that way because she knew that even though she was Timmy's first and she was his, the bond with Charley and the love that was always passed through them while they connected in a way that was stronger than ever could never die and it was always better then she had hoped or dreamed of. She knew that

Charley cared for her and loved her and so she walked down the stairs to the kitchen and started the coffee, she was about to grab two cups from the cabinet when a vision popped into her head and everything went black. She gasped for air as pain hit her and it felt like someone was punching her and then she felt blood running down her arms and mouth and when she looked like she was seeing what the person was seeing she was nothing but at the vision seemed like it was her she saw what the person saw and as the person kept getting punched and kicked she could see a man beating and kicking this kid in the middle of an alley. She looked even closer and saw that the boy was one of Charley's friends and he was a lone and tried to defend himself but the guy had caught him off guard. She tried to help the boy and tell him that she and Charley will be there soon, but the boy acted as if he was going to die and so she had to think fast and as the vision started to fade away, she raced up the stairs yelling Charley's name. When she saw Charley standing in the door alarmed and scared, she said, "Baby, one of your boys is getting beaten up really bad in the alleyway near the movie store." Charley grabbed a shirt and pants and quickly got dressed and so did she, she turned off the coffee pot and before too long they were out the door, they raced through the woods and as he ran in animal form and she raced through the trees never hitting the ground.

A lost soul. . ..

They reached his friend within seconds and the man was just
about to hit him on last time before he was surely about to die,
when Charley leaped in the air and latched onto the man's arm
and dug his teeth so far into him that the man couldn't get
Charley off if he tried. Blood started to trickle down the guys
arm and he yelled in pain as Charley dug his teeth even further
about to rip his arm off. Michelle stood there trying to figure
out what to do this man to repay back the pain and within a
couple of minutes she found the answer and so she starred at
him and searched for his thoughts and mind and when she
found it, she closed her eyes and made him suddenly be filled
with fire and pain and soon before she knew it his body crumbled
to the floor and he burned from inside out. She quickly ran to
his friend and knelt down beside him not sure how she could
save him. She had never really saved or healed a person before
but she was not going to let him die because of the man that
had some kid of kill streak going on, so she laid her hand on his
forehead and started to think of the pain and the cuts and
everything that the man did to him and how it never happened
and it faded away. After she released him, he gasped for air like
he had just come back from death and looked at her and then
at Charley who was now near her and hovering over the boy.
The boy laid back on the ground and said, "Thank you guys, I
thought I was dead for sure, I don't know what his deal was he
just came up behind me and started hitting me and I tried to
fight back and he could an advantage real bad." Michelle looked

at him and said, "I know honey, I saw in my vision and grabbed Charley and we raced here to save you" The boy smiled and then slowly got up and they walked with him and made sure that he got home soon, and then left. Charley was silent for a long time before she said, "Are you okay?" Charley looked at her and at first she saw hate and then his face relaxed and then he said, "I am now that he is okay, I wanted to rip that guy's body apart and then you did it for me and I still feel like I should have done it." She looked at the ground as they walked around the open streets and said, "I know I took action but I was looking out for you and him, I'm sorry It is what I do when you are not with me and you were kind of hanging there so I had to do something." He smiled at her and said, "I know you are always saving my neck, what would I do without you?" She smiled and said, "I don't know but I do know that I would go crazy without you" He laughed and then kissed her and pulled her close and then they walked to a coffee shop and sat down by the window and drank their coffee. Charley looked at her as she looked out the window and he could tell by her face that she was thinking of all the crime and the problems that she knew were ahead for her and he wanted to fix it and solve it all for her but he also knew that soon she will leave him and he had to prepare for it. He didn't want to think of it but he knew that she loved this guy Timmy and that this guy loved her and so he only had a few options, He could go to this guy and fight for her and leave her to deal with the crime or he could wait until this guy came and be by her side and help her fight the crime of the world. He didn't know how he was going to do it but he did know that he wasn't going to leave her ever. He drank his coffee and touched her hand and when she smiled, he smiled back and then he whispered "I love you" She smiled and looked down at his hand and hugged it tighter and then looked back at him and said, "I love you too". They finished their coffee and then the left the coffee shop and she pulled him into a diner that was very popular and they sat down again across from each other and ordered some breakfast and more coffee. They sat there in silence for a long time before she said, "So, what is on the agenda for today?" Charley smiled and said, "Well, we have to save the world don't we?" She laughed at the sound of it and then said,

"Well, I can only save what I see or feel, I don't know everything that is out there" He laughed and said, " I know it was a joke" She laughed and then smiled and then said, "After we eat we should walk in the park and then maybe the beach." He smiled and then said, "Sounds good, then we should take pictures and then maybe lunch and then watch a movie and then dinner I will cook for you" She smiled and then frowned at the thought of pictures and then she looked away at the outside and for the first time Charley could see the pain that was in her face and in her body language and he said, "What's wrong?" She turned to him and then said, "Nothing Charley" he tilted his head to her like a dog and then said, "Yes, there is what did I say?" And as he watched her and replayed what he said it clicked and then he said, "You and Timmy took pictures before he left didn't you?" she never turned her head to him she just nodded her head in a yes motion. Charley then said, "I see" She turned to him because of his tone and when she turned to him she could see the pain in his eyes but also the understanding. She said, "What?" Charley said, "Nothing?" She looked at him and then said, "What Charley?" He looked at her and then said, "Are you afraid that if we take pictures that you or I will leave?" She sighed at his question and then said, "It has crossed my mind, because I don't know what will happen soon, but I know that it will come down to either a happy ending or not and I don't what to lose you or him and I don't want you to leave me because I'm being stupid and making you feel like you're not worth anything because you are worth more than him at the moment but I know that when I see him that my heart will try to tell me different and I am scared." He nodded in understanding and then said, "Well, I am not going anywhere because I love you and you are mine and I will be your husband soon, and nothing will change that and I will fight for you and what we have if you will." She smiled and then said, "I love you Charley and will be yours forever and as long as I live and I will also fight for what we have as well as our love. He smiled at her and then said, "Than there is nothing to worry about then huh?" She laughed and then said, "I guess not, I told you that I was being stupid" He laughed and said, " No, you're not it is normal to feel that way with all of the memories and visions that seem to haunt you, but we will deal with it later but after breakfast we will walk on the beach and in the park and then take some pictures and then a movie and then I will cook you a nice dinner and then I will make love to you as long as I can okay?" she giggled and then said, "Okay, baby" When they turned the waitress was coming with their food and so they waited and then when the waitress placed their food in front of them and made sure that they were okay and didn't need anything else, then she left and they began eating their breakfast in silence. After about 10 minutes or so later, they finished their breakfast and then talked a little bit more and then Charley paid the waitress and tipped her and then they left hand in hand and then they headed for the park and went for a walk enjoying the fresh air and the animals and the people talking and walking with others. It was a peaceful day and joyful as well, then they walked down the streets and headed for the beach that was crowded with people swimming and playing sports and enjoying the day as the sun was shining and loving it all. They would normal drive to these places but for some reason since they weren't that far from each other they decided to walk everywhere. After they walked from one end of the beach to the other they took some pictures on the way and then some when they exited the beach and then they walked to the movie theater since it was still early and then afterwards they ate lunch and then took more pictures and decided to rent some movies even though they went to one in the theater, they just wanted to relax at home and so they rented some and then raced back to the house. When they got to the house they put in a movie and Charley began cooking as she sat on the couch watching the movie. She had this feeling that he was watching her while he cooked and so she had this idea and thought that it would get his mind off her and worrying about her and so she stood up and saw that he was looking at her. She slowly walked over and came up behind him and wrapped her arms around him and then slowly stroked his chest and then moved down to his belt and this made him breathe heavy while he was preparing dinner. She lightly giggled and then before she knew it he had turned around and pinned her against the cabinet and was kissing her. She giggled even more and then he threw off her shirt and his and then started to kiss her from her chin down and didn't stop and as he moved his lips over her, her body was going crazy and wanted him so bad that she couldn't take it anymore. She slowly whispered in his ear and said, "Take me now" He pulled his clothes off faster then she had ever seen him and she had done the same and before she could take another breath she felt the vibration of being connected with him and it was the best feeling she could ever dream of. She realized that for the first time the connection that she had with Timmy was never like this and nor would it ever be. She arched her back and her head and has they were one and moving in harmony she knew that no matter what happened in the end that her love for Charley was stronger than anything now as time went by. She looked down at him and saw that he was what she was looking for and not Timmy and so enjoyed every minute of this feeling until they were finished. He released her and she felt like a part of him was still inside her and she relaxed her body and then pulled her clothes on and watched him as he did the same. She noticed that when he moved it was more like caution and almost like he was hiding something from her. She saw that after he put on his clothes he turned back to what we was doing before they had started and then she said, "Charley why are you so tense and trying to protect yourself and hiding something from me?" He didn't turn around for a while and then he slowly turned and said, "I can't help wonder if every time we make love you think or compare me to him" She looked at him for a while and then said, "Charley every time we make love I have never compared you to him, or him to you, the other thing that I have ever done is understand the feeling that I feel at that moment or the other time and I realized this time that the feeling that I felt was stronger than with him and I know now that what we have is not weak and nor can it be changed." I sighed and then said, "I have realized who I cannot live without and who I need , as well as who I want to be with for the rest of my life, but I 'm not going to tell you who until I know for sure and that is all that I can do for now" She turned and walked away from him and went outside on the back deck and looked at the sun leaving the earth and getting ready for the moon to take over and guard the world from what it is. She noticed that Charley never followed her outside and he just remained where he was and never looking back and cooking.

Words Unspoken. . ..

She knew that it was killing him and hurting him, but she had to make sure that what she was feeling was the right way to go and she also had to make sure that whatever choice she made that she would not look back and wish she chosen the other one. She knew that it was going to be hard but at the same time it was even harder loving two people at the same time and hating one for hurting her and leaving her and forgetting her. So stood there for a long time before Charley came out and said, "Dinner's ready" She turned around to see that he was blank and no expression on his face at all" She walked in and sat across from him as they ate their dinner, she was worried that this was not good response but at the same time she didn't want to bring it up again. She kept silent and then when she was done she took his plate and hers and then put them in the sink and instead of sitting on the couch where he had sat she walked up stairs and lay on the bed in her clothes. She fell asleep really quick letting her brain adjust and to process everything that needed to be done. When she woke up the next morning she realized that Charley never came in that night and when she went downstairs to the smell of coffee she saw that he was no where inside. She fixed a cup of coffee and stepped outside to the nice warm morning with the sun shining and then she turned her head to the right and saw that he was in animal form and was running through the forest that was not that far from the house. She watched him as he ran and ran, she wanted to run after him but she knew that he needed this time to think and so she just stood there and watched him. After a half hour she went back into the house to fix her another cup and then fix one for him and she went back outside and saw that he was running toward the house in a speed that was faster then she could have ever seen him run. He stopped right in front of her in animal form and when their eyes met he looked at the ground and said, "Thanks but no thanks, I don't want any coffee I just came home to pack up some stuff and take a shower and then I am heading back into the forest for awhile." She put the cups on the railing of the deck and said, "Charley, why? You don't have to leave, I need you" He turned to her and said, "I need time to think and I think you do as well and I'm not going to sit here and fear that one day or soon that you will walk out of my life forever and so I'm going to live in the woods where I need to be, I don't know how long yet but I will howl when I decide to come back." She was shocked and hurt at the same time and she didn't know what to say to this or to him, so let him walk out the door with no goodbye or kiss and before she knew it she had the memory of Timmy leaving and the feeling of wanting to go after him and bring him back but she never did because she couldn't but that was then and this was now. She was not going to let Charley leave and never come back like Timmy. She decided that she would let him leave for now but tonight she would follow him and find him and make everything up to him. As the door shut and he raced into the trees and she never saw where he went after that, she knew that it was going to be hard to track him but she had skills and talent for it and so she got ready and packed her clothes for the journey ahead. She sat down at the table and decided to fix breakfast and so she ate it and then before she knew it she couldn't help it anymore because she knew that he could be half way around the world by now. So, she packed some food to last her a couple of nights and days and locked the house and took off on foot through the trees. She listened as she could hear everything and soon she heard the ground be pounded by paws but they sounded really far away and so she put her book bag on her back and took off running in the direction of the paws. It took her a good couple of hours and before she knew it, it was already dark before she went up a tree and looked down to see Charley lying by a tree in human form. She slowly crawled down the tree and walked over to him but she kept her distance just in case she alarmed him. She spoke firmly and strong as she said, "Charley, How dare you leave me and think that I would let you go without a goodbye or a kiss" Charley opened his eyes and looked at her and said, "How did you find me?" She laughed out loud and said, "please, We have been together for a long time now that I can feel you, see you, and hear you" She knelt by him and saw that he tensed up when she touched him and so she stepped back and said, "So, it's going to be like that huh?" She turned around and said, "Well, then if you don't want me near you or in your life then I will just move out all the way and you can have your house back and you won't have to worry about me and my problems or my love" She started to walk away and before she could reach a tree to jump into Charley grabbed her arm and turned her around and pulled her close. She pulled away and when he tried to pull her back she fought him and then he put his hand on her face and said, "Michelle, I don't want you to leave, I want you to be mine and to be my wife and to be the mother of my children but I can't sit here and feel the pain that you feel and the fear of knowing that you can't be mine, I would have come back but I just thought that if you had time to yourself, it would have been easier for you" She pulled away from him and looked at him with anger in her eyes, and then she spoke harshly and with rage and said, "Charley, do you not understand what you did back there, you did the same thing that he did to me, leaving me and never returning and making me get through life the best that I could and I realized after you left that I was not going to let you leave me and it end like it did when Timmy left." She tried to fight back the tears and then she said, "I can't do it again Charley, I can't my heart can't take it and so you can either come back to me and we will talk it out or you can stay here and if you don't come back then I will know that I no longer need to be here, it is up to you I have done what I can" She turned away and ran up a tree and left him standing there and watching her and when she reached the deck she couldn't fight back the tears again and so she started to cry harder then she had ever before. She buried her hands into her face and couldn't stop crying and what seemed like forever was only 10 minutes and when she looked up Charley was standing by a tree that exited the forest but opened the path way to the house. He walked slowly and calmly to her , and said, "I'm sorry I never knew that he left you like that and never came back, I always thought that he left and visited you but then after that stopped calling and all that " She moved her and head back and forth and said, "NO, he never saw me or called me after he left I had to live my life like he was never there and it was hard and it hurt so bad and I always wanted to go after him but I never did." Charley ran to her and pulled her hands away and lifted her eyes to meet his and then said, "So, you came after me?" She nodded and then he wrapped his arms around her and said, "I'm sorry my Michelle, I will make it my job to make it up to you for the rest of your life if I have too" She didn't smile but the feeling that she felt was warmth and love and without saying anything she took his hand and pulled him to the house and when she opened the door she pushed him to the couch and when he sat down, she didn't know how to say what she about to say and she knew that it was going to be hard and when she looked at Charley and his expression she knew that he was expecting the worst. She paced back and forth but after a couple of minutes she stopped and turned to him, she looked at him and then she knelt in front of him and held his hands and as she looked at him and his eyes met her. She felt a freedom and peace and hope and so she spoke without further a due and said, "Charley, you have been there for me from the beginning and fought for me without hesitations and gave me the love that kept me going and strong and now we are faced with a problem and as I sit here I have decided that I cannot lie to myself anymore or to you and so I have decided that from here on and I will tell you what I have chosen." Before she could continue Charley had pulled her up into his arms and kissed her firmly and then said, "I don't want to know, I trust you and this is something that you need to deal with and I will be right by you whatever your choice may be." She was confused but she saw his face and realized that he was going to be with her no matter what her choice was, and so she kissed him back and then said, "Okay" he hugged her close and as she still remained on his lap he played one of the movies that they never watched and soon after the movie was over he carried her up the stairs and into the bedroom to make up for the pain and for everything that he had caused her to let her know that he loved her more than anything. After he did what he knew would make it right to her she fell asleep fast and he laid there watching her and protecting her as she slept. Soon after watching her for awhile he drifted off to sleep and for once he was happy and content knowing that in the end she will be his no matter what. When he woke up the next morning he saw that she was still asleep and so he got up and put on his pants and then walked downstairs to start breakfast and the coffee, when he was fixing her cup he turned to the stairs to see her walking down them toward him. He handed her the cup and she smiled at him and then she said, "So, school today I guess we should get going before we are late" He nodded and then said, " I will take you and pick up" She nodded and then he finished some eggs and bacon and hash rounds that took some time but he got them done and they ate it at the table and then they took their showers and got dressed and then headed out the door an hour later and got into his car and then he started the car and then before she knew it they were heading on the road to school and the whole time she was wondering how today was going to be. She got out of the car after kissing him goodbye and entered the school doors feeling like it was going to be a new day and different. She went to all of her classes finding that each one was just as boring as the others and soon she realized that it has been over a year since Timmy and in a couple of months she would be graduating as well as Charley from his school. She wondered what would happen and what would become of them. Out of the blue she saw that the room went dark and everything vanish and then she could see her and Charley standing by a pastor getting married and it was in a couple of years and then she saw that his family was there and hers and they were happy and then she could see that they were living in a nice apartment and going to college and working and paying their bills and their life was the best and it was a happy ending. She came back to reality and found that the she knew this feeling and so she knew that her choice was the right one but she would keep it in until the time was right. When Charley picked her up that day, he was glowing and happy and so he kissed her excitedly and then said, "I have a surprise for you but I'm not going to show you until the weekend" She looked at him and said, "No fair, that means I have to wait 4 more days" He beamed and said. "Yep" He drove off and headed to his house and when they got there her mind was racing and trying to figure out what kind of surprise would he get her, I mean she already had a nice ring on her finger when he asked her to marry him and she said yes and she gets to be with him forever and everyday which is all she wants and needs. Her mind couldn't rest and so the next four days went by slow and dragging but as Friday came around she couldn't help it when he woke her up that morning and took her to school and tried to keep his mouth shut. She went to school excited and wanting to know so badly that she thought about ditching school but she knew that he would be mad. She waited the day and soon the bell rang and she grabbed her stuff that she would need for homework and ran to his car that was parked out front. When she threw her book bag in the back and buckled her seat belt he took off and around the school and he took out a blind fold and put it around her eyes so that she couldn't see. She looked at him and said, "NO Fair" He laughed and then said, "Almost there" After a couple minutes he pulled the car to a stop and then untied the blind fold and when she opened her eyes she saw the apartment that was in her vision and she smiled and laughed out loud. Charley looked at her and said, "What's funny?" She turned to him and said, "I had a vision of this and it was ours and we were married and happy together" He smiled at this and she could see that he was happy and then he said, "Well, this is ours because I just bought it with the money that I saved over the years and we can move in now." She wrapped her arms around him and kissed him and said, "Yes, now let's" He smiled and then took out her key and gave it to her and then took off from the parking spot and back toward his house and when they got there she saw that he had already got a truck and they loading it with everything that was his and hers and they were almost done. She turned to him and said, "Wow, you were busy when I was in school" he smiled and then said, "Well, I had to make a few phone calls while I was in school and they came when I got off which was early and then started packing everything and loading it up on the truck. But they will follow us soon and then they will unpack it as well into the apartment and I promise you will not have to lift a finger.

Dreams come true. . ..

She believed him and she cuddled closer to him and kissed him. She stood there watching the men work at packing everything in the truck and after a half an hour the man turned to Charley and gave him the thumbs up and Charley returned the gesture and so they got back into the car and took off toward the apartment again and when they got there the truck was backing up and parking near the entrance. Charley and Michelle got out and opened the front door and when she stepped in it was as it was in her vision and she could see a big kitchen that had a bar on the side with bar stools and straight ahead she could see a bedroom that was the master bedroom and then to the left was another bedroom and then the bathroom on the right and then a hallway but when she went to the left was where the kitchen was and then a living room. It was so cozy and beautiful that she wanted to cry out or happiness but she kept it together and when she turned around she saw Charley looking at her and his face showed concern from her response. She laughed and said, "NO, I'm okay, I'm actually happy not sad" He smiled and said, "Good" then he turned around to help the guys bring everything inside the apartment. After a couple hours of work they unpacked everything and got it to where they wanted and then it was even more beautiful than before. She saw her couch and his that was positioned just right to see the big screen TV that they had and then a computer desk in the corner and then a table that sat 5 in a space that was close to their kitchen near the bar stools and the kitchen was all set with everything that they needed in the place where they could reach it and find it easy. Their bed was a queen with nice sheets and comforters that were purple because that is what she wanted and they had two dressers with her clothes in one and his in the other. The closet was big and they shared it and then they had their own bathroom that just right for them. Then in the other bedroom she had put a another bed so that when someone came over they could sleep in it and or maybe one day it could be a nursery and as this thought hit her she turned to see Charley behind her and he was watching her. She said, "You got two bedrooms on purpose didn't you?" He smiled and then said, "Well, I hoped that one day we would have a child but I knew that it would be better to be prepared then not" She smiled and then said, "Charley it's perfect thank you" He smiled and then kissed her and then said, "Your welcome my love, now what would you like for dinner?" She thought about it for a minute and then said, "You know we should go out and celebrate" He nodded and then said, "Okay, sounds good, where would you like to go?" She laughed and then said, "Surprise me" He laughed at this and said, "Okay, Applebee's it is" They laughed as they left the apartment and locked the door behind them. As they drove to the restaurant they played music and sang along together laughing and happy and when they sat down in their seats at the restaurant enjoying each other's company and then she had this feeling that nothing could get any better and then she was surprised when everything went black and she tried to hide it from everyone but Charley knew what was happening and he jumped up and wrapped his arms around her and softly whispered into her ear comforting her and letting her know that he was there. And even though she could hear him she couldn't see him all she saw was Timmy walking down the street covered in blood and it was his own, then she saw a man following him with the weapon he used and Timmy taking off running trying to get away from him, She gasped out of response and then she could feel Timmy and his pain and his heart and how it was beating faster than ever and scared more then he has ever been and then she could feel the anger of the man that was following him and how this man had a revenge feeling from Timmy and that he wouldn't stop until he was dead and so she had to do something, she knew that she wouldn't be able to get to him in time so the only thing that she could do was destroy this man now and so she thought hard and evil and full of rage and what happened next shocked her as well as Timmy and Charley that was still holding her and hearing and feeling everything that she was. She said a curse under her breathe and in her mind toward the man and soon before she knew it the man exploded out of nowhere and Timmy looked back and when he saw this he took off running even faster thinking that he was next. But she said in her mind to him very softly and calmly, "Timmy it's me Michelle I took care of him so you are safe and can go with your life and whatever you need to do" She saw Timmy stop and as he heard his thoughts and knew that it was her he said, "Michelle, My love I am so sorry I never forgot you, I never stopped loving you I had to go in hiding for a long time because the girl that I was with ended up to be a crazy one and her father was in Mob and he and his men kept coming after me and my family, he killed everyone that I loved except for my father and me and of course you it seems, I thought that he killed you because he told me that he was going to come after you but I guess he lied or he hasn't tried yet." He paused and then said, "I'm so sorry I didn't know that this was going to happen and I don't know why it did in the first place because I didn't do anything to make him mad at me, but I'm glad that you are okay and I want to see you." When he stopped she said, "Timmy, I will never stop loving you and thinking of you, but I am with Charley now and he has saved me more times then you could ever imagine, if it wasn't for him I would have gone insane and I owe him so much these past couple of years and soon me and him are going to get married" When she said these words she saw Timmy turn around and he said, "Married, no you can't please Michelle I never meant to hurt you, I haven't forgotten our promise to each other and I never will and I want you to be mine and be my wife, please Michelle I love you and I can't be without you" She started to cry and then she felt Charley tense beside her and all that she could do was rest her hand on his and squeeze it harder than he ever imagined she could have as far as strength. She sighed and then said, "Timmy, I don't know what to tell you or what I feel right now, but I will let you know, Goodbye Timmy" As she started to come back to reality she heard him say, "NO, wait Michelle" and then he was gone and she saw Charley looking at her and then he went back and sat down across from her and then she noticed that there were some people looking at her and she looked down at the table and then back at Charley. His expression was very angry and hurt and then he said, "You know Michelle, I don't know what to do about this, I mean if he is telling the truth then you should be with him if you really love him, but at the same time I don't want you to go anywhere." She looked at him and then said, "I don't know Charley, I don't know what to do at all" She started to cry as their food came and the waiter asked her if she was okay and she nodded at him and then her and Charley ate their dinner in silence and then they went back to their apartment and when she entered the apartment she couldn't do anything but pace back and forth. Charley tried to hide his feelings from her and but as she paced she knew that he was hurting and angry. Part of her wanted to get in her car and drive to Timmy and straightened things out the best that she could but at the same time she didn't want to leave Charley in fear that he would leave and then she would never be able to see him or find him. She knew that what Timmy told her was the truth but at the same time she had let him go a long time ago even though she still loved him but the love was not as strong as it used to be. She also knew that in a couple of days her and Charley would be graduating from High School and then a week after that they would be starting their new jobs, Charley would be working with his father in his company and Michelle would be with her parents and so she knew that her life was going the way that it should for the most part and what she always wanted. She stopped pacing and then relaxed on the couch as Charley watched her in the thinking process and then he got up and kissed her forehead and went into the bedroom and shut the door and she knew that he was having a hard time with this and watching her. She relaxed against the couch and shut her eyes and before she knew it she was dreaming of the choices in front of her and she was thinking of the loss of Charley and the gain of Timmy as well as the problems that it would cause if she chose him and if what would happen if she chose Charley. It was hard but her heart was fighting her more than her mind was. As she was dreaming she started to see another vision but this time it had to do with a couple girls getting raped and beaten and so she knew that she had to leave and help them. She left Charley a note that said:

Dear Charley,

As I was dreaming and sleeping on the couch, I had a vision of some girls that were getting raped and beaten and so I think I'm going to take this time to myself and I should be home soon. I love you and don't worry about me I will be back. Love, Michelle

Then she exited the apartment and headed on foot down the road and toward where the girls were calling for help, When she got there she was so angry and full of rage that she killed the man worse than before when she killed and she brought the girls to the hospital and then started walking down the streets trying to clear her head and her thoughts and every time she got where she needed to be another person needed her and then she realized that with Timmy she would never be able to do what she needed to do because he would never understand and it wasn't like he could go with her and because what she does it dangerous and he would always get hurt or be a threat and so she knew that with Charley that would never happen because he could take care of himself and her and his boys. She kept walking and when she was able to breathe and no one else needed her she headed home and when she got there she saw Charley sitting on the couch holding the letter she left, she saw that he was concerned and then when he looked at her she could read his face and that worried her and then said, "Are you okay, I told you I was going to be back" He looked at her and then said, "I just got this , but when I first woke up I thought that you left me, and was angry but then when I read this I understood." She walked over to Charley and realized that she had been gone all night almost because the sun was starting to come up and then she knelt before him and said, "I'm sorry I didn't realize how long I was out, it didn't seem that long but every time I was able to think out everything someone needed me and when no one else needed me I came home to you." He took his hand and lifted her chin so that he could see her face and then he said, "It's okay, baby I know that you feel like you have to do this and sometimes don't need me, just promise me that you will always come back to me" she smiled and said, "Always" he bent down and kissed her and then he stood up and wrapped him arm around her waist and then said, "Let's get some coffee and breakfast and then we can go to school and then shopping afterwards and then maybe out to dinner and then who knows what else" She laughed at this and then said, "sounds good to me" So, they ate breakfast and drank their coffee and then he dropped her off to school and then she realized that today was Friday and that on Saturday there was going to be no more school for her or Charley and then she had this feeling that either Saturday or Sunday Timmy was going to come to her but she tried to get the thought out of her head and she went on with school like normal.

Worst Nightmare. . . . .

As she sat in class that day, she was feeling strange and was feeling like something was about to happen. She didn't know what but she knew that a war was going to happen soon, and so she tried to relax and concentrate but she couldn't no matter how hard she tried. Finally, after a couple times trying to concentrate and focus everything went black and she saw Alexia and Neptune talking in a old house that they had found and claimed and then she read their thoughts and found that they were planning to fight against her and Charley for killing their brother. She thought that this was not good but at the same time she was ready and so she listened and then when the vision started to fade away. She got up and realized that the class was starring at her. She acted normal and left without a word and then called Charley and told him what she just saw. Charley told her to stay in school and that he would get his boys ready and then he would get her after school. She didn't want to stay put she wanted to go after them and finish them off on your own. But she knew that Charley wouldn't let that happen, so she had to plan ahead and so she hung up the phone and took her books out of her locker and headed out the door. She got into her car and headed toward Georgia where she knew they would be. It took her hours but when she found the old house, it was dark and creepy but she hid the car and slowly got out dressed in her night outfit and when she approached the window, she saw that they were having a lot of people over and realized that they were the friends that she thought Charley killed before.

But as she looked closer she realized that these were very different from the others and so she knew that they had more friends then she thought before as well. She tried to get a closer look but before she could someone placed a hand on her shoulder and when she turned around ready to fight, she saw that it was Charley and he was mad, madder than he had ever been before. She tried to smile and then whispered, "I'm sorry, I was trying to protect you and them and didn't want to get you guys involved" He looked at her and said, "We are involved and this is our fight together not just yours." She nodded and then said, "Now, what?" He smiled and then said, "We attack" They went back to the forest to plan and then Charley decided that they were just going to invade and kill them all, it wasn't the best idea but he didn't care. So, when they waited for the time to be right one of his buddy's smashed down the door and when everyone in the house prepared themselves, it made it worse because the fight was starting and she knew that it would go for hours. She saw one of the witches' grab a friend of his and so she struck back and made the witch explode in front of everyone and soon they were aware of her and her powers and were starting to get scared but the brother and sister tried to give them confidence and to fight back. She saw two that was powerful as well and they grabbed one and tried to split him in half by their minds and before they could she made them burn from the inside and soon when he was released, he ran after another one that ran out of the house and into the forest. Charley didn't like him going alone and so he sent someone else to help him. Soon, they were up against a couple more at the same time and it was hard but he fought two and she fought two and soon she had killed them all and then soon they were getting closer and closer to the brother and sister. When the fight slowly started to slow down, they were outside in the back yard, and the brother and sister were the only two that were left and before they knew it they had Chad Richard's by the neck and they were threatening to kill him right there and then if they didn't back away. Michelle knew that Alexia and Neptune knew that the fight was over and that they couldn't win. Even though they had lost a couple dear friends, they would win in the end. Before Michelle could react or Charley they heard the scream come out of Chad's mouth and soon it stopped and Alexia dropped his body like it was trash and Michelle could see that Charley was getting mad and about to strike but she couldn't let that happen. She grabbed Charley and as he fought to get free from her, she held even tighter and when he realized that her strength was coming out and that he couldn't get free, he relaxed against her. She held her gaze to Alexia and Neptune and said, "That was not right, nor was it necessary" Alexia and Neptune laughed and then said, "Oh, but killing our brother was?" Michelle glared at them and then said, "Your brother kidnapped me and made me do things that were against my will, and so that was different" She saw Alexia and Neptune get mad and then they were about to strike her and Charley and so she let go of Charley and told him to grab his boys and leave them. Charley fought her on it but knew that he wouldn't win. He took off running and into the forest and then when he found his boys he told them to spread a part and watch the back yard and Michelle but to keep their distance and only attack when she needed them. Charley slowly crawled to the side of the house and watched through a bush and saw Michelle standing there only a couple feet away from the brother and sister and he saw that her body was tense and ready to strike with all force. He lay down on the ground in animal form and waited until she needed him. Michelle stood there knowing that Charley and the boy were close but she didn't want them to do anything because she was going to do something that she never attempted and didn't want any problems with it. She waited and then after awhile Alexia moved forward and then Neptune followed and they put their arms in the air like they were about to strike when Michelle put her power in full force and found that it was easier than before and soon she had Alexia and Neptune in the air and they were lifted from the ground like she had picked them up and held them in the air and they couldn't move. She stood there watching them as they tried to struggle and break free and when they found out that it was no use they knew that it was over and that they were going to die. Michelle was more powerful than they were and so she held them there wondering what she should do that would make it worth it or to make it even. She thought long and hard and then soon it came to her and then without further a due she said a spell in her mind and soon it revealed that they both had dangers in their back pockets and so the spell that she said was to make one kill the other. And so as she held them in place, she saw that they both grabbed the dangers and they both hesitated because they didn't want to kill the other but they had no choice and soon Neptune stabbed his sister and Alexia stabbed her brother and when they were no longer moving or breathing. Michelle let them down and they laid there motionless and she stood there feeling strange and like the hate and anger that covered her was trying to break free but she fought it off and then turned and said, "It's okay boys, it is safe to come out" Charley walked out and turned into human form and as he looked at her he said, "Michelle, what was that?" She looked at the ground and said, "I don't know Charley it just came out of nowhere" he looked at her and then walked closer and then said, "Are you sure that it is safe to come over to you?" She watched him and then saw that he could see her feelings and her face. She nodded and then said, "Yes, it is" when he reached her he grabbed her and she buried her head into his shoulder and then took deep breathes and then when he released her. She looked at him and he looked back at her. She tried to smile and so did he and then they kissed and when the boy came into view in animal form they barked and then ran into the forest back to their homes. They stood there for awhile letting everything sink in and then they walked around and headed out of the yard leaving them there. Michelle stopped and then said, "You know we shouldn't leave Chad there." Charley nodded and then said, "I will take care of it" He walked back and then picked up Chad and carried him to the forest and barked three times and she saw that one his boys stayed behind to make sure that he was taken care of and so she got into the car and waited for Charley. When he came back a couple minutes later, she started the car and drove out of the hiding place that the car was in. They drove for hours and when they finally got home, she saw a box on their doorstep and when she saw the name she gasped and said, "No way" Charley was soon beside her and said, "What?" Michelle could only point and there on the box was in big letters Trevor and it was addressed to her. She picked it up and it was heavy and when they got inside she wasn't sure if she wanted to open it but at the same time she wanted to know. Charley told her not too, but she didn't listen. She ripped it open and inside was a box in the shape of a heart and a letter. Inside the box was everything that belonged to her mother and father and much more. The letter said,

Michelle,

If you are reading this then that means that I failed and that I am no longer alive and the love that I felt for you was never there, I'm sorry for everything that I have caused you and Charley and I tried to make it right but it never worked. If you are reading this then if I was right then you have already killed me and my brother and sister and this is not what I wanted to happen at all. But since I cannot give you this in person since I am dead I have sent this to you beforehand so that you can know about your parents and to know the truth and to love them the best you can. I am sorry and hope that this helps.

Trevor

She read the letter a couple of times before passing it on to Charley and then she looked down and saw that it had pictures of her parents growing up and her it seemed like they had kept tabs on her since her parents died because it had pictures of her from the time she was a baby until now and it was kind of creepy to her but at the same time she just looked at them with Charley and then she put them back in the box and hid them in her closet. She came back and sat down next to Charley and then cuddled up against him and knew that everything was going to be okay for now on. She kissed him and then after awhile he got up and went into the kitchen and made dinner and before the movie started she relaxed against the couch and tried to make everything disappear that had happened. Charley called from the kitchen that dinner was ready and she slowly got up and sat across from him and started to eat in silence. She saw that he was looking at her and he said, "Are you okay?" She tried to smile and then said, "I think I will be" They smiled at each other and then they finished their dinner and then did the dishes together and then went back into the living room to watch the movie that they had been waiting for. She cuddled closer and as the movie started she slowly drifted off to sleep and soon Charley held her tight and kissed her on the lips and didn't move as she slept peacefully and relaxed. But as the movie started to be a blur Charley also started to fall asleep, dreaming and ready for the next day.

Promised action. . ..

After a couple weeks went by and Charley and Michelle was getting used to their new life together on their own and working with their parents. Michelle found that the business was a rough place to be and trying to keep up with everything but she was a smart girl and knew that one day she would own the company. But she knew that Charley would always be there for her and would be home when she did and that she could cuddle with him and love him and that everything would be right again once her heart healed and let go. Charley also found that working with his parents was hard and more challenging then he had thought but it was always worth it, because he knew that when the day was over he was going to see the woman that he loved and that stood by him no matter what. She worked until 5 pm that night and when she drove home she had this feeling that Charley was already home and when she opened the door she saw him in the kitchen and he was cooking dinner. Charley turned to see her standing at the door watching him or so he thought, but as he looked at her he knew what they look meant. Charley ran to her and held her close and soon she was trying to hold on to him so that she wouldn't fall and then as Charley had her and was starting to get worried he tried to keep her steady and standing but her body fought him and soon she just dropped to the floor and she let out a scream and Charley picked her up and sat her on the couch and then tried to comfort her but she just kept shaking her head like she was trying to get rid of the image in her head. She took a deep breath and then she said, "You know that I will help you Timmy but this is all that I can do, after I help you I will be done with you and it, I can't keep doing this to me and you and my Charley" Charley listened and then she said, "I need you to get me all the information on her family that you can and I need you to fax it to my house now" She listened and then said, "It is 243-678-9002 and when I get it then me and Charley will take care of everything okay." Soon Charley could see that she was coming back and when she did, he looked at her and said, "What happened?" She looked at him and then said, "Remember when I told you about the girl that tested me and I showed her and I told her that if she ever hurt him or his family or mine I would kill her" Charley nodded his head and then said, "Who?" Michelle sighed and then said, "She went to her father and lied to him saying that Timmy hurt you and was using her and so her father killed his grandmother and almost killed his father" Charley helped her up and said, "You wait for the fax and I will finish dinner and then we will plan what our next action is next" She looked at him and then said, "Charley, I know that you want to help me but I think that I should do this by myself" Charley turned to her and said, "No, I am going with you" She started to argue and then stopped and then said, "Okay, but please If we get to the point where it is better for me to kill them let me, because I can do it faster and without a trace" Charley nodded and then went to the kitchen and finished cooking his pasta and chicken parmesan and bread to go with it. After 15 minutes later the fax came in and so she grabbed it and brought it back to the table and on it, were all the 20 names that was in her father's Mob and then it had her mother and her and her father as well. The names were so long and strange but she gave it to Charley and said, "We go down the list, but I have a feeling that they will all be at the warehouse on Elk street where I have seen some well dressed men go every Thursday. Charley nodded and as they finished eating, they left in a hurry and when she drove to the warehouse but parked her car a street over, they watched as the men got out of a nice Lincoln and they watched as they saw that they were carrying heavy weapons, one was an automatic pistol and then one had a semiautomatic and a few were loaded with revolvers. She looked at Charley and said,

"This is going to be a close one and might be hard but we can do it" Charley nodded and then said, "Let's go around the back" She agreed and then they slowly got out of the car and headed to the back of the warehouse and since it was dark they were lucky because no one saw them. They entered into the warehouse and walked through the smelly hallway that had pipes everywhere and rats as well. When they got to where they needed to be, they saw all of the men crowded around a table that was kind of round and then they heard them talking about them killing the rest of Timmy's family and love ones and she was shocked when she heard her name. She turned to Charley and said, "Wait here, I need to approach them first and then you can come and help" Charley hesitated but then nodded because he knew that she could take them all out in one strike. She walked down the stairs that led to the room where the men were and said, "Well, guys I hate to invade on your plans but I don't think that you will be killing me tonight" One of the guys stood up and he seemed to be the leader and he said, "Who are you?" Michelle smiled and said, "I am Michelle" She waited for it to register and then when she saw all the guys get up, she waited until they started to come after her. She was shocked that they didn't try and kill her but then she knew why it was because they wanted to use her as bait and then kill her later. But she knew that it was never going to happen, she laughed at this thought and then before they got closer she had all of them in the air and flying. She saw two of them look in fear and one look like he had seen a ghost and this just brought happiness to her. She held them there and thought to herself what should she do. Before she acted she sensed that Charley was beside her and then she said, "Well, darling what should do to them?" Charley looked at her and then said, "I don't know what do you think?" She thought about it and then she started with the first one and searched his thoughts and then soon he was forming bumps and bleeding out and soon when his heart stopped beating he hit the floor. The others were starting to get scared and not sure they wanted to see the next one get killed. She didn't stop there she went to the next one and then the next and soon after she had killed each one with a different death she released her power and relaxed. She turned to Charley and said, "Now, let's take care of the rest" He followed her out of the warehouse and they ran into a guard that was outside and before she could react to it, Charley had bit him and killed him. They quickly ran to their car and took off driving down the road toward the girl father's house. When they reached the house and saw that it was a big white house with too many rooms and doors but it was rich like the family and they slowly crept into the house and found that the girl was in her room and her parents were in theirs. Michelle walked toward the parent's room and swung it open, she saw a very heavy set man sitting on the bed with nothing but boxers and a white tank top and he said, "Who the hell are you and what are you doing in my house?" She laughed and said, "Oh, My name is Michelle and I believe that your daughter has talk about me a few times" She saw that he knew and then he said, "Oh, so you're the freak" Michelle didn't like that at all and when she saw the father go for his gun that was in his bed side table she had him pinned against the head board and then when the mother came in she screamed and then Michelle pinned her against the wall with her mind and her hands free. She thought about doing what she did with the brother and sister of Trevor but she knew that they deserved more than that. She thought for a minute and then she set the father on fire and then the mother. She let go and then walked out with Charley next to her and they walked up the stairs and when they got there they saw the girl coming out of her room to see what was happening and when the girl saw her she took off running in the other direction. Before she could turn the corner Michelle had her pinned against the wall as well. The girl begged and pleaded with her but Michelle looked at her with no pity and hate and said, "Why should I spare your life when you put mine in the hands of a killer and the rest of my family as well as friends" Then she saw the girl turn evil and then said, "I would do it again, because you and your friend are nothing but scum and don't deserve to live" Michelle heard Charley growl behind her and then she said, "Well, I told you that I would kill you if you did anything to hurt Timmy or my family or his" and so she growled at the girl deep down in her throat and then without knowing or feeling she tore the girl in half and when she heard her heart stop she released her. Michelle felt anger and hate but at the same time peace now, she didn't know why but she did. She also knew that she would never be able to bring Timmy's grandmother back but she knew that she did the best she could. Her and Charley left the house fast and smoothly and then when it was safe she called Timmy and when he answered he said, "Hello" She sighed and then said, "Okay, Timmy they are gone and you don't have to worry about it or hide no more" Timmy was silent and then he said, "You killed them all how?" She smiled and then said, "Well, Timmy that is for me to know and you to wonder" Timmy was silent and then said, "Really, tell me" She sighed and then said, "Timmy you knew from the start that I was not like you, and so I am a witch and can do things that you would never imagine but it doesn't matter now you and your family are safe." Then she said, "I have to go now, take care and maybe one day we will hang out as friends" Timmy tried to talk some more but she hung up and then looked at Charley and saw that he was tense and she said, "What's wrong my love?" He looked at her and then said, "I never knew that you could be so evil and hateful" she laughed and then said, "Only when I am mad or really really mad" He laughed and then said, "well, hopefully I will never make you mad or really really mad:" They laughed at this as they drove down the road and back to their place. She wanted to forget everything and she wanted to cuddle up with Charley and love him all night long.

The Happy Ending. . ..

The whole day she couldn't stop preparing herself for when Timmy came and took the life that she had and put a gap in the middle and she was trying to find every method of choice that could either save her from having to make the choice but she knew that she was not going to be so lucky. At the end of the day of school she walked to Charley's car and put her book bag into the truck and then slowly climbed in and then kissed Charley with a smile but before he drove off he looked at her and said, "Hard day?" She smiled and then said, "Boring and challenging but I know that tomorrow will be better when it will be over." He smiled and then drove off and she sat there thinking of everything that needs to be done and what she needs to do to prepare herself. They went to Wal-Mart and bought some things for the apartment and then went to dinner a couple hours later and then he brought her to Belk's and then TJ Maxx and bought her some clothes and other things that she wanted, she felt like a princess that night and then he gave her some money and it was more then she could have asked for but he gave it to her and said, "Baby, I want you to spoil yourself with whatever you want, so when we go back home take your car and go pamper yourself and when you come back I will have a surprise for you" She didn't know what to say but she took it and then looked down and counted it and it was over $200 and so she kissed him and then said, "Thank you" He drove them home and then she grabbed her coat and purse and the money and went for a drive and was trying to think of what she could do for herself that night and so she went and got her nails done and then her hair cut and colored an auburn color. When she was done she didn't know what else to do so she decided to go back home and when she entered the apartment she smelled the aroma of roses and vanilla and when she turned the corner she saw something that was wrapped and sitting on the kitchen chair and it looked big enough to be a picture of some sort. She saw rose petals sprinkled around the room and she saw Charley sitting on the couch waiting for her, when she looked at him she saw in his face a love that was deeper then she could have dreamed and when he slowly got up from the couch and walked to her she knew that what he was seeing was the new her. He walked over and placed his hands on her cheeks and he kissed her passionately and then moved back and said, "Wow, baby you look beautiful I love the new look" She smiled and then kissed him back and then she turned to the gift and said, "What is this?" He smiled and said, "Something that I found and thought that you would like it since I know you love wolfs and Indians" She walked over and tore the wrapper to reveal a beautiful frame with an Indian girl and her wolf next to each and gazing at a moon in the distance and the colors were what made her stare and she loved it and could look at it forever. She turned to Charley and kissed him and said, "Baby, I love it" He smiled and then unwrapped it the rest of the way and then turned to the wall that was above the couch and hung it up and then stepped back to see it. She smiled next to him and then said, "It's beautiful and then they sat down on the couch and then watched some TV and then before she knew it, she fell asleep laying on Charley and when she woke up she knew that today was going to be a busy day and stressful. She got up and didn't wake him and then took a shower and made coffee and she wore a white shirt and a short black shirt with comfortable but pretty black dress shoes that had a heel but it was thick and she knew that they would have to do. She woke up Charley and when he saw her he thought that he was late but she put her hand on his chest and said, "You still have time, I just wanted to get ready early" He nodded and then said, "Okay" He took a shower and then got dressed in khakis and a dress shirt and then dress shoes and they drank their coffee and then since they had time they decided to go to breakfast and so they went to Captain Table's and when they were finished He drove her to her school and then he drove to his. It was kind of sad because her family and she would be at hers and Charley and his family would be at his and they wouldn't be able to graduate together but it was how it had to be but they made plans to meet up at a restaurant afterwards so that they were all together. When she walked across the stage to retrieve her diploma she knew that her life was going to be better and full of wonder as well as challenges but she was prepared for them. She took pictures with her family and friends and then after her goodbyes to everyone she went with her parents and the rest of her family which were uncles and aunts and cousins and they headed to the restaurant that they had chosen which was cheap enough but had good food and she sat by Charley and everyone was having a good time and enjoying family time. When they were done and the family split the bill for her and Charley, Charley and Michelle went in his car and drove back to their apartment. They were excited but at the same time relieved that it was over and now that they could relax and do what they wanted. When they got inside they cuddled on the couch and kissed each other a couple times before he said, "Well, now the only step left is the wedding" She turned to him and saw that he was being serious and then she laughed out loud and said, "Yep, that's the only thing left to do" He kissed her and then said, "When?" She looked at him and said, "Ummm...Remember we planned for August 16th and since we have everything planned and taken care of, we might as well do it" He looked at her and said, "Wow, you are not giving yourself much time there sweetheart, and your funny" She smiled and said, "I know but sooner the better" She kissed him and then got up and went into the bedroom and when she closed the door she leaned against it and took a deep breath because she knew that it was going to be hard for her in the next couple days but she was ready now and she knew what she had to do. But her heart was pounding and hurting at the same time and it was so loud that it felt like it was going to come out of her chest. She took another deep breath and then changed into her comfortable clothes and then went back out into the living room to see that Charley hadn't moved and he was sucked into the TV screen again. She laughed and then said, "I swear you and that stupid TV, you know maybe you should marry it instead of me" When she saw Charley's expression and his face said Not funny she laughed even harder and when she saw that he was not laughing she walked over to him and wrapped her arms around him and said, "Baby, it was a joke" He tried to smile and then he said, "I'm sorry I just got this really strange feeling that came over me and I'm trying to understand it' She looked up at him and then said, "Like what?" He gazed at the screen of the TV but he wasn't watching it though she thought he was and when he looked away he turned to her and said, "I don't know how to describe it, it's sad but it's angry and then happy" She looked at him and then she said, "Is it your feelings?" He smiled and said, "NO" She looked at him and though she knew that he could feel other people emotions she was wondering if it was hers that he was feeling but she wasn't angry so it couldn't be. She looked at him and said, "Well, what else is there?" He turned to her and then said, "I don't know, but I do know that it's a boy and he's close but he's keeping his distance until the right time so I don't know." He snapped back to reality and then said "I'm sure it's nothing" He got up and kissed her then he moved to the kitchen and called over his shoulder and said, "What do you want to do about dinner since we had lunch at the restaurant?" She looked at him and said, "I don't know but we just ate didn't we?" He said, "Yeah but I just wanted to prepare for it when the time is right to cook it" She smiled and then said, "Okay" Then she said, "Well, we could go out or you can fix whatever you baby" Charley looked at her and smiled and then he said, "You shouldn't have said that" Then he laughed but he took out a couple steaks and then made sure he had potatoes and a vegetable and then he went back to sit down next to her. They watched TV until 5pm and then he got up and cooked dinner and when they were eating dinner at the table, she noticed that he was not paying attention to anything but the feeling that was overwhelming him. She touched his hand and said, "It'll be okay Charley" He looked at her and then said, "I hope so" They finished their dinner and then he kissed her goodnight and said, "I love you" She told him that she loved him back and kissed him and then he went into the bedroom and shut the door. She sat there on the couch confused and not sure what to do when her phone rang and she realized that it was on vibrate but she looked at the ID and there was no name but she answered it and said, "Hello" She listened for a minute and the voice on the other side made her clench the couch and it was warm and soft and she knew it anywhere. Very calmly the voice said, "Hello, My Love I know that we have a lot to talk about but I really need and want to see you so we can talk, can you meet me at the top of the bridge at midnight?" She didn't say anything and then she said, "Fine" She hung up the phone and grabbed her coat, she didn't tell Charley and didn't want him to worry but she knew what she had to do and since it was only 7pm now she had a couple of hours to walk the streets and help as many people she could before she met him. She quietly walked out and headed down the streets and found that a man was outside of a bar and he had cheated the bartender and so he was getting beat up and so she tried to help him but for the first time when she got there that the man was already dead and she couldn't do anything about it. She tried to bring him back but for some reason she couldn't and so she went on and found a child being chased by a dog and the dog almost got the kid but only bit him and so she made the dog go away, but she kept remembering Charley being with her and helping her. She was thanked by the child and then kept walking and before she knew it after helping the people that she could it was midnight. She walked up the bridge leaning on the railing dressed in her night outfit that she always wore under her clothes and always changed into in a private place that she created then in her own home. As she leaned on the railing she had this feeling that told her that he was close and soon she could smell him and feel him and when she turned around he had his hand stretched out like he was going to touch her. She pulled back and then said, "What do you want Timmy?" Timmy put his hand back and then said, "You" She looked down at the floor and said, "Well, you're a little late for that, and I guess you will never know" She turned to walk away and he tried to stop her but she pulled away and then turned around and said, "You know I waited for you and was true to you and never hurt you, and I know that you had to do to stay alive and whatever else but Dang it Timmy I'm getting married and I love Charley and you had your chance, and I'm sorry, I will always love you but that was in the past and this is now" She started to cry and he ran to her wanting to hold her and said, "I'm sorry to, I wish I had come to you when this stuff started and maybe it would have been different but I thought that if I left you alone and didn't let them follow me here that you would be safe but I didn't know what I would be giving up either or I would have not listened to my stupid gut" She buried her face into his chest and felt the warm embrace that she always loved about him and the feeling that he gave her but with him it was like she had to hide what she was and with Charley she could be herself and so she pulled away and said, "I'm sorry Timmy, I have to go" He tried to pull her back to him and then he said, "Please Michelle, don't leave" She kept shaking her head No and then she pulled back and he was no longer touching her and she said over her shoulder "I will always love you Timmy but it is better this way, I'm sorry" She walked into the night and disappeared into the trees and before he could say anything else she was gone.

Epilogue...

A couple months later it was August 16th, the biggest day of her life, she was standing in her bedroom that was once hers when she was little and she was looking at the mirror that she used to dress up and play girly. She starred at the person in the reflection and saw a beautiful woman that she didn't recognize but yet she was dressed in a white Dress with her hair up and make up that made her look like a Queen and she smiled as today was the day that she became Mrs. Barks and it was going to be wonderful and the best day and years together that she could have ever hoped for. Her mother was standing by her with her best friends as her Brides Maids and her Best friend that was Carla was her Maid of Honor and they were helping her get ready and to not be scared, which she was beyond belief. But she knew that what she was doing was what she wanted and no one was going to change that. She had let Timmy go for good and she was happier then she could ever be. She stood there being able to relax and breath and picture her life with Charley and being the mother and wife that he needed as well as wanted and then she remembered that it was time and her father was waiting for her and so she stepped away from the mirror and her mother said, "Honey, you look beautiful and Charley is a wonder man, your father and I are so proud of you" She smiled and then kissed her mother on the cheek and then she took her hand and she knew that her father was with Charley and so her mother led her out the bedroom door and through the hallway, when she looked down she saw the staircase that was draped with white ribbon and satin with white bows from start to end and then as she walked down the stairs she saw roses everywhere as well as ribbon and as they got to the back door her father took her hand and led her outside and there she looked forward and there at the end or you can say beginning with the minister and everyone that loved them was on the right and the left of her. Her father walked her down the red carpet aisle and soon Charley gazed at her with such love and ready to be hers and soon he looked at her and said, "You are so beautiful" He took her hand helped her up the steps to him and when She stepped up and stood by him, the minister began and said everything that was just right for them and then they said their vows and soon she was putting the ring on his finger and expressing her love for him and then he was doing to the same thing and then after their I do's and they kissed for the first time as Husband and Wife. Charley and Michelle turned to the crowd and bowed and then walked down the aisle and since the back yard was big and they had a band playing on one side they were able to dance with everyone in the family and then they ate with friends and family. Soon, after everyone left they went back into the house and changed their clothes and then came back out with their suitcases and ready for their honeymoon. Charley packed their car and then helped her into the car, they said goodbye to their family and friends and then drove off into the Sunset with the new life that was ahead.